"I can honestly say been the cause of any wedding being called off."

"I can't believe it."

"It's true." But there was something about the way he was looking at her that was so warm and flattering that it made her feel as if she actually might have the power to turn the heads of other women's grooms.

And suddenly, out of the blue, she wasn't imagining him holding her hand or putting an arm around her the way she had been earlier. She was imagining him kissing her....

Which was totally inappropriate.

He's a client, she shouted in her mind.

And she was on hiatus from men!

But still, there she was, looking up into eyes that made her feel beautiful, that made her feel as if no other woman in the world existed. And yes, she was picturing him leaning over that car door and pressing his supple mouth to hers....

Wondering what it would be like...

Wishing he would...

Dear Reader,

Vonni Hunter is the wedding planner who can't find a husband. And she's tried. Since college she's devoted herself to hunting for one, and put everything on hold to do it. It's exhausted her and left her not only still single, but without any of the other things she wants in life either. So she's taking a break, having a little Vonni-time, and temporarily swearing off men.

Confirmed bachelor Dane Camden has two goals with Vonni—plan his grandmother's wedding, and convince her to work for Camden Superstores as their own private wedding coordinator.

Dane's devotion to bachelorhood is well-known and not something Vonni questions. For now she's not in the market for a husband, anyway. So, unveiled and without any risk of anything personal developing between them, Vonni and Dane come together.

Only there just might be a little risk after all. And some fun taking it...

Happy reading!

Victoria Pade

A Camden Family Wedding

—

Victoria Pade

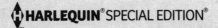
HARLEQUIN® SPECIAL EDITION®

Recycling programs
for this product may
not exist in your area.

ISBN-13: 978-0-373-65807-7

A CAMDEN FAMILY WEDDING

Copyright © 2014 by Victoria Pade

Printed in U.S.A.

Books by Victoria Pade

Harlequin Special Edition

^Fortune Found #2119
**Big Sky Bride, Be Mine! #2133
**Mommy in the Making #2162
**The Camden Cowboy #2194
§Corner-Office Courtship #2217
§A Baby in the Bargain #2254
§It's a Boy! #2276
¶¶The Maverick's Christmas Baby #2301
§A Camden Family Wedding #2325

Silhouette Special Edition

Willow in Bloom #1490
*Her Baby Secret #1503
*Maybe My Baby #1515
*The Baby Surprise #1544
His Pretend Fiancée #1564
**Babies in the Bargain #1623
**Wedding Willies #1628
**Having the Bachelor's Baby #1658
∞The Pregnancy Project #1711
¤The Baby Deal #1742
**Celebrity Bachelor #1760
**Back in the Bachelor's Arms #1771
**It Takes a Family #1783
**Hometown Cinderella #1804
**Bachelor No More #1849
¶A Family for the Holidays #1861
**The Doctor Next Door #1883
ΔDesigns on the Doctor #1915
**Hometown Sweetheart #1929
**A Baby for the Bachelor #1971
ΩTexas Cinderella #1993
**The Bachelor's Northbridge Bride #2020

**Marrying the Northbridge Nanny #2037
**The Bachelor, the Baby and the Beauty #2062
**The Bachelor's Christmas Bride #2085

Silhouette Books

World's Most Eligible Bachelors
Wyoming Wrangler

Montana Mavericks:
   Wed in Whitehorn
The Marriage Bargain

The Coltons
From Boss to Bridegroom

*Baby Times Three
**Northbridge Nuptials
∞Most Likely To...
¤Family Business
¶Montana Mavericks:
   Striking It Rich
ΔBack in Business
ΩThe Foleys and the McCords
^The Fortunes of Texas:
   Lost...and Found
§The Camdens of Colorado
¶¶Montana Mavericks:
   Rust Creek Cowboys

Other titles by this author available in ebook format.

VICTORIA PADE

is a USA TODAY bestselling author of numerous romance novels. She has two beautiful and talented daughters—Cori and Erin—and is a native of Colorado, where she lives and writes. A devoted chocolate lover, she's in search of the perfect chocolate-chip-cookie recipe.

For information about her latest and upcoming releases, visit Victoria Pade on Facebook—she would love to hear from you.

Chapter One

"See? The gifts for the attendants are wrapped, I've confirmed your hairdresser, the caterer and the florist, and we have a guarantee that the cake will be ready and delivered on time. I'm working on the place cards tonight. I promise you, absolutely everything is under control and it will be a truly amazing wedding!"

Vonni Hunter made sure there wasn't the slightest hint of haste in her voice as she spoke to her client. It wasn't uncommon for one of her brides to panic as the wedding date approached. But this bride had shown up unannounced at Burke's Weddings' offices twenty minutes before closing time, and Vonni was in a hurry to get to an after-hours appointment. Not giving that away in her tone, she asked, "Is there anything else I can do for you?"

"Yes. You can make me look like you in the next four days. I need to get rid of the extra six pounds I've gained from stress eating!" the other woman wailed.

It was Monday. This particular wedding was being held on Saturday. The bride was the daughter of one of Denver's most prominent men, and while she'd been a pleasure to work with, she was a large and not particularly attractive woman on whom six more pounds was not easy to see.

But, as luck would have it, she'd stopped by the dress designer for a surprise visit today to try on her gown. Although the final fitting had been done weeks ago, the dress no longer fit and would have to be altered again. That had induced the panic that had brought her here to Vonni.

Vonni looped her arm through the bride's and tugged her closer. "Melanie, you are the woman Douglas fell in love with," she reminded her. "He got down on one knee and asked you to be his wife—do *not* forget that—"

"But you're blonde and beautiful...." the bride lamented.

"And someone who can't get a man to propose if my life depended on it!" Vonni confided with a laugh. "Not once. Not one man. Ever. No matter how much I've wanted it or how hard I've tried—and believe me, I've *tried!* I'm the wedding planner who can't find herself a husband. But you, Melanie Danforth-Hayes, in four more short days, are going to walk down the aisle to the man who loves you like nobody's business, and become Mrs. Douglas Barnes. And then the two of you are going to party your little hearts out to celebrate that. It's *me* who's jealous of *you!*"

The round-faced bride broke into a slow smile and blinked back the tears that had been threatening to fall. "He does love me. Just the way I am," she conceded. "And *he's* gained ten pounds—we have to have more alterations done on his tux. That's what got me to think-ing that maybe I should try the dress again."

"And you did because fate is smiling down on you and now the dress won't be a problem. Everything will be just perfect," Vonni assured her again, thinking that she was glad two last-minute disasters had been avoided because it was much easier for her to make a few nips and tucks with her emergency sewing kit than to get a bride and groom into clothes that were too small.

"You always make me feel so much better," her bride said, obviously beginning to relax.

"I just want you to have a fabulous wedding and a long and happy life with Douglas," Vonni said honestly. "You deserve it."

"So do you. Well, not with Douglas, but you know, with someone else."

Vonni laughed again. "From your lips to God's ears," she said. As they'd been talking, she'd slowly moved her client to the front door, which she now opened. "And as always, if there's anything you need or get worried about—"

"I know I can count on you. I'm sorry for this meltdown—of course you have everything under con-trol. You've done every wedding I've been to in the past few years and they've all been fantastic."

"And yours will make those pale in comparison. You've made some of the best choices I've ever seen and it's going to be just wonderful."

"I think so, too," the client confided. "I know at least three people who are going to be green with envy."

Vonni laughed again. "We'll make sure of it."

And she had her out the door.

They exchanged goodbyes on the sidewalk in front of the shop—located in the heart of Cherry Creek North among the more elite boutiques—and Vonni went back inside alone.

It was already past closing time, so she locked the door behind her, and then rushed to her office.

It wasn't unusual for her to be asked to accommodate clients by going to them rather than having them come to her. The lion's share of clientele for Burke's Weddings was Denver's rich, and they were accustomed to being catered to. But being asked to go to the Camden Building to see Dane Camden was a unique situation.

First of all, although there had been several engagement announcements for members of the Camden family in recent months, Dane Camden's wasn't among them.

Second, as a rule, Vonni met with the bride, the bride and her family or the bride and groom together. She'd never met with a groom alone. At least not for the initial appointment.

And third, when Dane Camden had called to make the appointment, he'd said that not only did he want to talk to her about a wedding, he also had a proposition for her that was better discussed away from the shop.

Being propositioned by a groom was definitely not the norm.

Although he had amended his description to a *business* proposition with a deep, surprisingly appealing chuckle.

There was that Dane Camden charisma she'd heard about.

No doubt, Dane Camden had charisma to spare.

But not enough to make her forget the cautionary tale of the Hunter family's past dealings with the well-known Camdens. Vonni was leery of any *business* proposition he had to offer.

With very few minutes to spare, she went into the office that technically belonged to Burke's Weddings' owner, Chrystal Burke. But since Chrystal was rarely there, Vonni considered it hers.

As she crossed the expansive space to the private bathroom, she thought about what it would mean to do a Camden wedding. It would be a feather in her cap. And lead to a lot more business. It would help pave her way to the promised partnership in Burke's Weddings that had long been her goal.

So this was an appointment she intended to keep, as soon as she did a quick check of her appearance.

Today, she'd worn the sides of her blond hair pulled back into a clip, and it was still neat and tidy. But she ran a brush through what was left to fall loose to her shoulder blades.

Her mascara and eyeliner were still in place, accentuating her green eyes to good effect. She freshened her blush, reapplied her mauve lipstick and blotted away the slight end-of-the-day shine from her nose and chin with a piece of rice paper.

Like everyone, there were things about her appearance that she was self-conscious of. She thought she had too much forehead but she looked awful in bangs so couldn't wear them to diminish it, and she knew that when full lips went out of style she'd be back to wearing pale lipsticks again to hide hers.

On the whole, she was okay with her appearance, though. Certainly she didn't see anything awful enough in it to scare away men. But she hadn't been lying to her client when she'd said she'd had no luck finding a husband of her own despite her every attempt. And she *had* made every attempt.

Early in college something had clicked in Vonni and

she'd realized that what she really wanted in life was to get married and have a family. That while a career was nice and she'd fully intended to get her degree and find one, in her heart of hearts, it was the traditional route that called to her—becoming a wife and mother. Picturing herself without that had seemed empty and sad and unfulfilling.

That was when she'd launched what she called her husband hunt.

And she'd been devoted to it ever since. It had been a mission, a passion, her main goal.

But going after something—no matter how keenly—and getting it had proved to be two different things.

"So you really do have one up on me, Melanie Danforth-Hayes. A very, very big one...." she said out loud.

But there was no time for thinking about something she'd already dedicated more years and energy and thought to than she wanted to admit—something she had now put on the back burner. Something she *needed* a break from. So Vonni tucked her tan shirt firmly into the waistband of her brown slacks and put on the short jacket that matched the pants.

She looked businesslike. That was what she'd set out for and what she'd accomplished.

She swiped a tissue across the toes of her three-inch-heel pumps to make sure they were clean, and hurried out of the bathroom to the oversize antique desk in the office.

She kept everything she needed for an initial appointment in a leather binder. She took it out of the top desk drawer, took her purse from the bottom drawer and went back through the shop and out the front door again.

The Camden Building was three blocks down the

street from her and it was a lovely June day, so it was silly to drive. But she walked at a fast clip to not be late.

When she reached the twelve-story yellow brick office building and went in, she headed straight for the reception desk and told the security guard there that she had an appointment with Dane Camden.

"Top floor."

Of course....

The Camdens owned the building; where else would they be?

After several people exited the elevator, Vonni got on alone and pressed the button for her floor. On the way up, she thought about the man she was about to meet.

She had no doubt she would recognize Dane Camden even though they'd never met. She'd seen him in the occasional photograph accompanying the newspaper and magazine articles about the Camden family. They owned the worldwide chain of Camden Superstores and any number of businesses and manufacturers that supplied them, so they tended to be high profile.

And Dane Camden himself got around. So much so that she'd seen him in the background of several snapshots her brides had shown her—incidental to copying his date's hairstyle or something else they liked and wanted to use for their own weddings.

Certainly his name had been dropped numerous times between brides and their bridesmaids. Being with him seemed to be some sort of rite-of-passage among the wealthy socialites who formed the majority of Burke's Weddings' clients and the entire circle of Chrystal's friends. Vonni had even overheard one bride laughing with her bridesmaids about how she'd had her turn with Dane Camden so she thought she might as well get married.

Despite the fact that he was a player, though, Vonni had never heard a single complaint about him. No one seemed to have thought there was any chance of getting him to the altar; there were only accolades for any time spent with him, and fondness and affection for the man himself.

"If anyone can show you that men and dating aren't all bad, it's him," one bride had said to her sister, telling her she needed a "hit" of Dane Camden to remind her how good it could be to be with a man again after a bad divorce.

So he was a bit of a legend. At least that was how Vonni had come to think of him.

The elevator stopped two floors from the top for a mail boy to get on pushing a cart. After that brief delay the doors closed again to finish the ascent.

What would it mean to the single women in Dane Camden's circle if he'd thrown in the towel and actually *was* getting married, she wondered then.

Not to mention who might have reeled in such a big—and elusive—fish....

When the elevator reached the top floor and the doors opened again, the mail boy charged through them, nearly knocking someone out of the way.

Someone who happened to be her potential client.

Dane Camden.

Who was remarkably better looking in person than in any of the pictures she'd seen of him....

"Vonni Hunter?"

"Yes," she admitted, wondering if she should let him know she knew who he was or wait for him to introduce himself.

But there was no wait.

"I'm Dane. Our receptionist for this floor left for

the day so I thought I'd meet you out here and save you having to figure out which office is mine."

"Thank you," she said, surprised that someone with this guy's clout would be that considerate.

"Let's go on back," he suggested. "Can I get you something? We have coffee, tea, soda, water...."

"No, nothing, thank you."

"I really appreciate you coming to me," he said as he ushered her into a plush corner office and motioned to the sofa against one wall instead of the chairs that faced his huge mahogany desk. "As I mentioned in our phone call, one of the things I want to talk to you about shouldn't be discussed at your place of business."

Vonni sat down on the edge of the couch, hugging the arm, as Dane Camden took the matching chair across the small coffee table from her.

Almost immediately, there was a knock on his office door and a woman who resembled him poked her head in. "Hey, sorry for interrupting, but you have to take a look at this before I can go home," she said.

"Vonni, this is my cousin January—we call her Jani. Jani, this is Vonni Hunter."

"Nice to meet you," January Camden said.

"You, too."

"And, oh, do you have the most beautiful green eyes in the world!"

"Thank you," Vonni answered, a bit taken aback by the compliment that was not at all businesslike.

"You're the wedding planner. I got married on the spur of the moment in a judge's office or I would have begged you to do a wedding for me. Maybe you could branch out into baby showers...."

Vonni merely laughed, unsure by the look of the

other woman in the loose-fitting sundress if she was in the market for that.

"But, Dane, I really do need you to—"

"I know," he said to his cousin before pivoting back to Vonni and aiming some pretty incredible blue eyes at her. "You'll have to excuse her. Jani is pregnant and using it against us to get her way," he said good-naturedly, obviously teasing Jani and confirming that a baby shower was likely on the horizon.

"Doctor's orders," Jani said with a beaming smile.

"This will just take a minute." Dane went over to his cousin, who was still standing in the doorway, and looked over the papers with her.

The two were engrossed in whatever it was they were dealing with, which gave Vonni the perfect opportunity to study the infamous Dane Camden and try to figure out why he was sooo much better looking in person.

There was no denying that in every picture she'd seen of him he was an attractive enough man. But the real thing? Wow! So much better....

His brown hair was a tad lighter than his cousin's— dark brown but the rich color of chocolate rather than espresso. He wore it short on the sides but a touch longer on top where it had just the right amount of wave to make him look sporty and casual but not unkempt.

She'd already noted the remarkable Camden blue eyes—and they were remarkable. It was another thing her brides and attendants swooned over when they were discussing him, and now she could see why.

Blueberry blue—that was what they were, Vonni decided. And penetrating and intelligent and warm and kind and surprisingly open for a person in his position.

But after more study, Vonni concluded it was his nose that made the difference between the way he looked in pictures and in person. He had a thin, long-ish nose with a bit of a bump in the bridge before it narrowed and slid down to a slightly squarish tip. It didn't photograph well, but was somehow very sexy in real life.

Overall, his face was lean and angular and very mas-culine, complete with lips that weren't at all full but were still so sensual they alone could chase fuller ones out of fashion at any moment.

He wasn't a refined kind of handsome, Vonni de-cided. He was more a rugged, outdoorsy, approachable kind of handsome.

The kind that got to Vonni.

And it didn't help that the face and hair weren't all he had going for him. He was also tall and trim, but with enough muscle to fill out both the sleeves of his gray suit coat and the thighs of the matching pants. Plus his shoulders were wide, his back was straight and he looked strong and healthy and virile and...

And altogether terrific.

There was just no denying it, even though Vonni wished she could because she should never be looking at someone else's groom and thinking how very, very hot he was....

"Nice to meet you, Vonni," Jani said then as she turned to go.

Vonni jolted slightly out of staring at Dane Camden, unaware until that moment that the two had finished with their business.

"You, too," Vonni said, as if she hadn't been lost in the unwelcome stirrings aroused by cataloging every square inch of the woman's cousin.

"Say hey to Gideon," Dane Camden said to January

Camden before he shut the door behind her and headed back to Vonni. "Sorry about that."

"No problem. And congratulations, by the way—I should have said that right off."

"For what?" he asked, his high, boxy brow wrinkling with confusion.

Vonni laughed, thinking that he must be new to his situation. "Congratulations on your engagement."

It was his turn to laugh. "Oh, I'm not getting married. Not me. Not now. Not ever. Never!"

He seemed very determined.

"But of course you'd think I called you to talk about my own wedding," he concluded.

"Well…people don't usually call me about other people's weddings…."

He laughed again—it was a deep, genuine, sexy sound that resonated through Vonni in a way it had no business doing.

Because even if he wasn't the groom, it didn't make any difference to her. Great looking or not, she was on hiatus from her too-long husband hunt. Plus, she'd learned the hard way not to waste time with commitment-shy men—and Dane Camden had just confirmed his reputation on that score. Quite resolutely.

"No, I'm sure they don't," he said then. "But this time that's what's happening. It's my grandmother who's getting married. And she wants it done in two weeks. That's why she called me—I'm the guy around here who gets the impossible done."

It took a moment for what he'd said to sink in.

His *grandmother* was getting married. Not any of the other Camdens whose engagements had recently been announced.

"You want me to do a wedding in two weeks?" Not

just a Camden wedding, but one for the matriarch of the entire Camden family....

"Yep," he confirmed. Then he grinned. It went slightly lopsided and put lines at the corners of his eyes and brackets alongside his mouth, and it just sucked her right in....

"Jani is right, you *do* have the most beautiful green eyes and they just got so big...." he said as if it delighted him. "They're the color of jade. Dark jade-green...."

And he was staring into them so keenly. So closely. So thoroughly....

But just as Vonni was getting uncomfortable he went back to what they'd been talking about.

"The wedding in two weeks," he said, more as if he was dragging himself back into the moment than as if he was reminding her. "Don't run scared. I think between the two of us it's doable because we aren't talking a spectacular production. GiGi—that's what everyone calls our grandmother—only wants a small wedding at home."

"How small?" Vonni asked cautiously.

"Maybe a hundred guests. Including family, which... I haven't done a recent head count and it's growing, but I'd say we're about a quarter of that number. And GiGi doesn't want anything too fancy or elaborate. Low-key, tasteful. She and her fiancé are seventy-five and neither of them wants a lot of hoopla. They just want something nice. And you won't have to worry about the ceremony—that will be in the den with only family looking on—so that cuts down on the preparations, too."

"But it's you I'll be working with?" Vonni asked, unsure if she liked that idea, since the man seemed to have a strange effect on her.

"GiGi is in Montana taking care of a friend who had

surgery. She can't get back until just before the wedding but this is the date they want—it's when they started *going steady* in high school. I'll be texting her and sending her pictures of everything, but yeah, you'll be working with me because it goes hand in hand with the other part of what I wanted to talk to you about today, which is my special project...."

"The business proposition?"

"Really slick how I got that in there, wasn't it?" he joked, laughing at himself. "Anyway, let's talk about that. We've decided that we want Camden Superstores to offer wedding packages. It's always been our goal to be a one-stop shop and now we'd like to introduce wedding departments to each of our stores to add that—"

"Wedding departments?" Vonni parroted, unclear about what this had to do with her. Then she became alarmed—did he want to learn from what she did for his grandmother's wedding and use it for his own *special project?* Camdens was notorious for undercutting and driving other companies out of business.

"Are you talking about selling wedding gowns? Bridesmaids' dresses? Tuxedos?" Things that she could recommend clients use Camdens for but that wouldn't take any of her business away....

"I'm talking about everything," he answered. "Clothes, yes, but the whole deal. Everything you do, too."

Oh, wonderful. And then she could be up against all of Camden Superstores....

"We want to offer packages that range from inexpensive to very elaborate," he continued. "From soup to nuts, including venues we can either contract with or that we might buy outright for rehearsal dinners and receptions. We'll provide decorations, tables, chairs, plates and silverware, linens—whatever's necessary. We can offer catering through our food departments. Cakes through our bakeries. Liquor through our liquor department. Flowers through our in-store florists—"

"Everything," Vonni summed up.

"And because you're known to be the best at what you do, we'd like to hire you to spearhead the whole thing."

That had not been what she'd thought he was going to say, and Vonni wasn't sure she'd understood correctly.

"First you want me—through Burke's Weddings—to do your grandmother's wedding in two weeks—"

"Right."

"And then you want me to *spearhead* the formation of wedding-planning departments in Camden Superstores to put you in direct competition with us?"

He shook his head. "Well, yes, there would be competition, but Camdens wouldn't be competing against *you.* I'm asking you to leave Burke's Weddings to come on board with Camden Superstores. You'd be the division director, responsible for completely designing and developing wedding departments with us that would be uniquely you."

"I'd come to work for Camden Superstores?"

"Yes. With the kind of contract we give our highest executives, including one of the best golden-parachute clauses around."

Vonni went from worry to disbelief in a nanosecond.

"You want me to quit Burke's Weddings—where I've been promised a full partnership—to become an employee of Camdens?"

Apparently her tone had alerted him to how unlikely she was to consider that.

"You wouldn't just be an *employee*. What we're talking about is making your name a signature brand. And you'll be in an executive position," he repeated. Then more somberly he said, "I know there might be some bad blood here."

The unsavory dealings between the Hunters and the Camdens went all the way back to 1953. Vonni hadn't been sure coming here today whether or not this generation of Camdens would know what she knew. Apparently Dane Camden did.

"But try to keep in mind that it wasn't a Camden who did the dirty deed—" he said.

"It was the Camdens who benefited from it."

"So did—"

"Yes, I know," Vonni cut him off.

"I'm just pointing out that we didn't have a hand in what went on," he insisted. "So couldn't you put aside what happened all those years ago? Especially since what I'm offering you is an opportunity for something much bigger and better than a *potential* partnership at Burke's Weddings. What I'm offering is a bird in the hand...."

As if her partnership wasn't.

Now he was making her a little mad, and the involuntary cock of her head must have alerted him to that fact.

"We want the best here," he said before she had a chance to comment. "And when it comes to wedding planners, you're it. We've all seen your work in weddings we've gone to. We know your reputation. And we know that you *are* Burke's Weddings. But it's Burke's Weddings getting the real credit."

"And with you it would be Camdens getting the credit."

He shook his head. "No. With us, you'll be the draw. People will have to come to Camdens to get a Vonni

Hunter wedding. From high-end to lower-end—even couples who couldn't otherwise afford a Vonni Hunter wedding will be able to get more conservative packages *designed* by Vonni Hunter, with Vonni Hunter's eye, with Vonni Hunter's taste, with Vonni Hunter's expertise. Brides who can afford you will get more personal attention—and with us that could be not only Denver brides, but celebrities and European royalty that we'll send you off to do first-class. What we want is to bring you into the spotlight, give you credit. And all the perks that go with it."

Okay, so it was flattering. And an intriguing idea. Enough to rid her of that small wave of anger.

"So you're going to put all the world at my feet as a wedding planner if only I can pull off a wedding in two weeks for your grandmother?" Vonni asked.

"The job offer is on the table no matter what. And we're figuring that if anyone can pull off a wedding in two weeks, it'll be you and me working together. I told you, around here I'm the guy who gets things done, and from what I understand, when it comes to weddings, you do, too."

Reminding herself that planning a Camden wedding would look very, very good for her, Vonni said, "Doing any kind of wedding for any number of people in two weeks is a push. But since I already have long-standing relationships with everyone it will take to accomplish it, it can probably be done. But as for the other—"

It was terrifying to think of what could become of her existing job if Camden Superstores did what he was proposing. But it was also completely unnerving to think about turning her back on Chrystal and Burke's Weddings to sign on with the Camdens and then ending up with nothing the way her grandfather had....

"Don't say anything about the business stuff for now," Dane Camden advised, interrupting her spinning thoughts. "We'll have plenty of time to talk about it. You can grill me, and negotiate, and tell me everything about it that might worry you, and shape it into exactly the kind of deal you'd feel most comfortable with. And if you need to yell at me or slap me around to feel better about what happened with your uncle and your grandfather and the way things turned out on that front, you can do that, too."

Oh, but when the man grinned it made her knees weak....

"You're not afraid that slapping you around might be pretty tempting?" she asked impudently.

"Just say the word. I'll get the gloves and you can beat the hell out of me."

She couldn't not smile at him. Although she made sure it was reserved. There was just something about him, and she could see how he got away with being the player he was.

"But you'll do GiGi's wedding with me one way or another?" he asked.

"That I'll do," she conceded.

"Then why don't you come up with a get-started list and we'll—" he shrugged one of those broad shoulders "—get started."

"I have two weddings on Saturday and this week is my race to the finish line for them both, so I'll have to do much of this after-hours—like this meeting."

"I'm open to evenings if you are."

"And the weekend—after the weddings on Saturday, and Sunday..." she said as if challenging him to back out.

"I'll be available whenever you can fit me in."

"Okay, then. I'm already swamped tonight working on place cards for five hundred but hopefully sometime tomorrow or tomorrow night I'll come up with the list and a schedule that we will *have* to stick to. Maybe we can meet again on Wednesday night?"

"I'll clear all decks."

"Then I guess we'll do a wedding. In two weeks."

The grin again. "I guess we will," he confirmed.

Vonni took her business card from her binder, along with her standard contract for him to look over, and the printout of what her services entailed.

Then, with nothing more to discuss at that moment, she stood to go.

"I'll show you back to the elevator," Dane offered, and she again had to give him points for courtesy.

While they were retracing their steps through the outer office, he said, "And when you're not thinking about my grandmother's wedding, think about your name on signs in every Camden Superstore—"

He raised an arm and swept his big hand across an imaginary banner. "Weddings by Vonni Hunter," he said as if reading what the signs would say.

But Vonni had had an entirely different sign in mind for years now. Stylishly painted in script letters on the shop's front window, *Burke's Weddings* would be replaced with *Burke and Hunter Weddings.*

She didn't say anything, but he must have sensed her lack of enthusiasm for his offer because as the elevator doors opened and Vonni stepped inside and turned to face him, he said, "Just think about it. And let me know when and where Wednesday."

"I will," she answered, pushing the button for the lobby.

Then as the doors began to close, he cocked his head to one side and said, "Wow. Yeah. Beautiful eyes…"

Which was strange because that was exactly what she'd been thinking the minute she'd turned and looked straight at him—how terrific looking he was and what beautiful blue eyes *he* had.…

But then the doors closed completely and the elevator began its descent.

She was thinking about Dane Camden on the entire ride down, though.

And how she could definitely see his appeal.

Even if she had no intention whatsoever of tapping into it.

Chapter Two

"How can you be so hard to get hold of when you're taking care of a sick friend in Northbridge where there's next to nothing to do?" Dane had finally connected with his grandmother after four calls to her cell phone the next morning.

"Oh, Dane, I'm sorry. We needed to take Agnes to physical therapy so that's where I was, and I forgot to bring the cell phone with me when we left," Georgianna Camden explained. "Is anything wrong?"

"No, everything's fine. But if you're gonna make me put on a pinafore and do your wedding like a girl, then you have to at least be available, Geege," he chastised, using his particular pet name for her.

"You're wearing a pinafore? *That* I'd like to see," she said with unabashed glee.

"I figure that's next since you've given me a job one of the girls would be better at. You know I'm not ever going to have a wedding of my own, so it isn't as if I've paid a lot of attention to what goes on at them. And now you want me to *plan* one? Come on, *me?*"

"Jonah and I are doing just fine, thanks for asking," GiGi said, ignoring his complaint.

Jonah Morrison was GiGi's fiancé, a man she'd known since they'd both grown up in the small Montana town of Northbridge.

"And how's Agnes?" Dane asked, knowing he was being cautioned not to venture too far from the manners his grandmother had taught him.

"She's doing well. Her knee replacement was a success and she's even getting out of the wheelchair to use the walker a little."

"Tell her hello for me and that she'd better be ready to get out on the dance floor for your first anniversary."

GiGi laughed and relayed both messages to her friend.

"Agnes says she'll be ready," GiGi repeated, though he'd already heard the seventy-nine-year-old herself in the background.

"I guess if I'm going to have a first anniversary, that must mean I'm getting the wedding when I want it?" GiGi asked.

"I met with Vonni Hunter last night and she says it won't be easy, but yes, she'll do it. I still don't understand why you want me to organize it," he persisted. "I don't know anything about weddings. I don't even pay attention when I go to them, I just look for the bar."

"And whatever single women you can pick up," his grandmother muttered.

He laughed. "That's what single guys do at weddings."

"Sorry, but I elected you to be my proxy," GiGi said remorselessly. "Just let the wedding planner guide you."

The prospect of being guided by the delicious Vonni Hunter did make the situation more palatable. But he wasn't going to admit that to his grandmother.

"Planning my wedding," GiGi went on, "will teach you what goes into the process and give you some background for setting up the stores' wedding departments."

"Developing the wedding departments is business. That I can do. And I'm fine taking my turn at making amends for old H.J.'s wranglings." H.J. was H. J. Camden, Dane's great-grandfather and the founding father of the Camden empire. "But all the frilly details for one specific wedding—"

"When have you ever known me to be *frilly,* Dane?"

The thought made Dane smile despite the fact that he was in protest mode. His grandmother was a tough cookie and she was right—there was nothing frilly about her.

Still, he liked giving her a hard time. "This stuff is frilly all on its own. Better suited to the girls than to me."

But his grandmother was adamant. "It's you I've asked," she said with finality. She obviously had no doubt that he'd do it—how could he deny any request from the woman who had taken him and the rest of his siblings and cousins in to raise when they were orphaned by a plane crash that had killed their parents?

"Okay, but if you end up with cigars as wedding favors, it's your own fault."

"There will not be cigars as wedding favors. There will be little bags of candied almonds—five in each bundle for good luck."

"See? That's not something I know about—"

"Which is why we have a wedding planner. Now tell me about Vonni Hunter," GiGi commanded.

"Jade-green eyes." Dane said the first thing that popped into his head.

"Jade-green eyes..." GiGi repeated. "They must be pretty...."

"Remarkable," he confirmed matter-of-factly. "She also has long blond hair, flawless skin, the kind of perfect nose that women usually pay for, though I think she was born with hers, lush lips that catch your eye and a petite, trim little body with just the right amount of curves to complete the package."

"So you hardly noticed what she looks like?" his grandmother goaded.

Oh, he'd noticed all right....

The woman was a knockout, and even though he didn't usually go for blondes, she'd hit all the right notes for him. So much so that the image of her had lingered in his mind since she'd left his office last night, even when he was thinking about other things. Even when he'd closed his eyes to go to sleep—there she'd still been in living color, making it tough for him to drop off.

But it didn't mean anything.

"I'm describing her to you strictly to let you know that if I can get her on board, she's beautiful and we won't have any problem at all putting not only her name but also her picture on all the promotional material," he informed his grandmother. "The way she looks will be a good marketing tool to go along with her track record as a wedding planner. So she'd be the perfect person to head our wedding department even if we weren't trying to compensate her—as the last remaining Hunter—for H.J. buying stolen goods and helping to give her grandfather the shaft."

H.J. had long been suspected of using any means necessary to get what he wanted. The recent discovery of his journals had confirmed for the family what they'd hoped wasn't true—that H.J. had been unscrupulous in his business dealings.

It was something the current Camdens were intent on making amends for. But in order not to incur a multitude of frivolous lawsuits, they were trying to atone for the misdeeds quietly, on the sly, without drawing too much attention or bringing the worst of H.J.'s behavior into the limelight.

"I see," Dane's grandmother said facetiously. "Memorizing every little detail about the way Vonni Hunter looks was purely business related."

Nothing got by GiGi. Her tone let him know she was fully aware that he was attracted to the wedding planner.

But that still didn't mean he was admitting anything. "Yep," he said, not letting her get a rise out of him. "I'm just looking ahead to marketing and advertising."

"Sure you are."

It was true, though. Regardless of how struck by Vonni Hunter he might have been, for Dane, women were just for fun. And he didn't play and work on the same field.

Plus there was the unsavory connection between the Hunters and Camdens in the past—he would never get mixed up with someone who could have any kind of ax to grind.

So there were two reasons he wouldn't let anything happen with her.

"I'm just telling you, Geege, that if matchmaking is what you have up your sleeve with this, don't run the risk of me screwing up your wedding for it. The past few of these assignments may have gotten some of us coupled up, but it isn't going to happen to me."

And Dane didn't have so much as a shadow of a doubt about that.

Yes, his younger brother Lang and cousins Jani and Cade had met their mates on these restitution projects atoning for H.J.'s sins, but Dane was going to break the pattern.

And for a third and very good reason over and above the fact that he didn't mix business with pleasure and that there was history with the Hunters.

He wasn't *ever* getting married or having kids.

As one of the three eldest Camden grandchildren, he felt as if he'd already been domesticated to death. He'd been answerable to GiGi, to his great-grandfather and to Margaret and Louie, the household staff who had been involved in raising them all. He'd done plenty of adapting and compromising. He'd helped care for and look after and teach so many younger siblings and cousins that he felt as if he'd already *been* a parent.

And now he just wanted the blissful quiet and sanctuary of living alone in his own house.

He wanted not to keep anyone's schedule but his own.

He wanted company when he wanted it and not when he didn't.

He wanted the perfect freedom of a single man who was *not* a parent.

So no matter how green Vonni Hunter's eyes were, it wasn't possible for her to get to him any more than she already had.

"I do not have *matchmaking* up my sleeve," GiGi objected. "I need my wedding planned. I decided it was you who should handle making things up to Vonni

Hunter, and the wedding departments were just my suggestion."

"Uh-huh…" Dane muttered at her feigned innocence.

Because he knew his grandmother. He knew that she wanted all of her grandchildren to get married and have great-grandchildren for her. And he also knew that while his cousin Jani might be newly married, pregnant and on a lighter work schedule, either of his sisters could have also been given all three of these projects without any problem. And certainly, they both would have been better suited to planning GiGi's wedding than he was.

"I'm not getting married, Geege. And no woman on the face of this earth is going to change that. Not you, not Vonni Hunter or anyone else."

"That's fine," GiGi claimed loftily. "You'll just be Poor-Old-Uncle-Dane-Who-Doesn't-Have-Anyone."

Dane laughed. "How about if I'm just Fun-Uncle-Dane-Who-Doesn't-Have-Anybody-Tying-Him-Down?"

"Finding a woman you love and having a family lifts you up, Dane. It raises you to a higher level and makes you a more well-rounded person. It's what we're put here to do."

"And your opinion wouldn't be at all colored by your own romance, would it? Plus, I've found a woman to love—more than one—you and Jani and Lindie and Livi—"

"Me and your sisters and cousin don't count."

"And I have plenty of family to lift me up and raise me to a higher level and make me about as well-rounded as I'll ever be."

"Kids you have with a wife—that's the family that elevates you and makes you complete," his grandmother persisted.

"I'm complete just the way I am. And happily single. *Forever!*"

GiGi's sigh on the other end of the line was pronounced, but Dane decided it was time to end this back-and-forth and return to the work he had to do. So he said, "I'm supposed to meet with Vonni Hunter tomorrow night to get started. So keep your cell phone with you—you never know when I'll have to call or text or send you pictures for approval. And we don't have any time to spare."

"I feel the same way about you," she muttered.

"You love and adore me no matter what I do with my life?"

"Yes," she confirmed begrudgingly. "I just don't want you to be a lonely old man."

"Couldn't happen in this family," he said, before saying goodbye and finally getting off the phone.

He was resigned to accomplishing all his grandmother had asked of him—short of getting personally involved with Vonni Hunter, which was not going to happen.

"Sorry, GiGi," he muttered as he set his cell phone on his desk. "The best I can do on the personal side is enjoy the view."

Of the lovely Vonni Hunter.

Who could not change his mind about marriage and family any more than any other woman could.

Vonni was standing outside the Cherry Cricket at eight o'clock Wednesday night when she spotted Dane rush out of the Camden Building a block down.

Neither of their schedules had allowed for an earlier meeting, and since the rough-and-tumble bar and grill was between their offices on Second Street, Dane had suggested he buy her a burger as they began the process of planning his grandmother's wedding.

Vonni had hesitated. She'd found it unnervingly difficult not to think about this guy since she'd met him, and because of that she knew it was better to keep this strictly business. A burger at the Cricket hardly qualified as being wined and dined, but there would be dining and she didn't want anything about her contact with him to seem date-like.

But he was very persuasive.

Plus, she knew she wouldn't have the chance to eat before they got together and didn't want her stomach rumbling through a business meeting.

So there she was, watching the intensely attractive Dane Camden coming toward her.

He was tieless, the collar button of his white shirt was unfastened and his suit coat was slung over one shoulder. He very much looked as if he was done with business for the day and ready to relax. Like on a burger date.

Luckily Vonni was still wearing what she'd put on this morning for work—a white cowl-necked blouse under a teal green jacket and pencil skirt with the toes of her four-inch heels pinching to remind her she was still working even if he wasn't.

"I didn't keep you waiting, did I?" he asked as he approached, flashing a smile that was enough to make her forget about her aching feet.

"I was a few minutes early." Which she always tried to be when it came to business. And that was all this was, she reminded herself when he held the door for her, told the bouncer sitting on a stool in the alcove that they were two for dinner then ushered her with a hand not quite touching her back to the table when the bouncer passed them off to the hostess.

All very date-like.

He requested a table outside where it was quieter and the hostess took them beyond the noise of the bar to a café table in the patio section that ran alongside the building.

Then the hostess traded places with a waitress who asked if they would like something to drink.

Before answering, Dane said to Vonni, "I'm having an end-of-the-day beer. How about you—beer, wine, something harder...?"

Vonni shook her head and spoke to the waitress. "I'll have a lemonade."

Dane ordered his beer and the waitress pointed out the menus that were stashed in the handles of a caddie that held ketchup, mustard, hot sauce and liquor ads.

"I'm starving," he said, grabbing the menus and handing one to Vonni. "Let's decide what we're eating so we can order when she comes back and then we can just talk."

About his grandmother's wedding, Vonni said to herself to neutralize the effect of his very casual attitude. And his appeal. And the feeling that this *was* a date.

But it wasn't! she reminded herself yet again.

Vonni focused on the menu, and by the time the waitress returned with their drinks, Dane ordered for them both, not forgetting a single detail of how Vonni wanted her burger or what she wanted on the side, proving just how attentive he'd been even as he focused on deciding his own meal.

Attentiveness that would have gained him points if this *had* been a date.

"Okay," he said when the waitress had left. He

reached around to the breast pocket of the suit coat he'd draped across the back of his seat and withdrew some folded papers. "Here's the contract—signed, sealed and now delivered."

He handed her the Burke's Weddings contract she'd given him to look over.

"The deposit check is there, too, to get the ball rolling."

Vonni glanced over them both and meticulously put them in a pocket of her leather binder.

"Now let's talk turkey instead of burgers," he suggested.

Vonni outlined the to-do list and the pace at which it would have to be done, then opened her date book to sort through some very tight scheduling.

"It's June—prime wedding month—and I'm booked to my eyeballs," she warned.

"Anything that works to fit us in. I'm completely at your disposal," he assured her, and he meant it because he agreed to everything she laid out for him—including evenings and the weekend.

"So," he said when they'd gone through it all by the time their burgers arrived, "we'll be seeing a lot of each other...."

"Until the wedding, yes, we will be," Vonni qualified.

He smiled as he checked out his bacon-and-blue-cheese burger. "Is that my limit? GiGi's wedding? If I haven't convinced you to come on board with Camdens by then will I have lost you for good?"

Leaving Burke's Weddings and working for Camdens—that *should* have been what she'd thought about since meeting him. But somehow every time it had come to mind, so had he, and she'd just ended up thinking about him.

A really good reason *not* to accept his offer....

"I'm happy where I am and doing what I do," she hedged.

"Great bargaining chip!" he proclaimed, sounding undaunted.

Then, just when Vonni thought he was going to launch into more sales pitch, he instead said, "We don't know much about the man responsible for our makeup line. Tell me about him."

"My grandfather?"

"And how he came up with formulas for makeup."

"Seriously?" Vonni said, doubting that he was genuinely interested.

"Seriously."

One of Vonni's big turnoffs on her manhunt had been men whose attention wandered when she talked. Certain that would happen with Dane Camden, she decided any kind of turnoff was a good thing. So she said, "My grandfather was a chemist. Well, he'd actually just graduated with a degree in chemistry when he was recruited into the army during World War II. He was put to work creating skin camouflage."

"Camdens' award-winning makeup line began as war paint?"

"That's what I was told. When my grandfather came out of the army—"

"Abe—that was his name, right? Abe Hunter?"

"Right. When he came home he had some trouble getting a job. My grandmother had read an article about Max Factor and she actually came up with the idea that my grandfather adapt his formulas for camouflage into makeup that women could use. You didn't know this?"

"Until recently all we knew was that once upon a time there was an obscure brand of makeup that my grandmother and my mother and my aunt all used and loved. So when my great-grandfather—H.J.—decided to add a makeup counter to Camdens stores, that was the brand he wanted to carry. And he bought the formulas for it in order to produce it, too. That's it. That's all that any of us knew until… Well, like I said, recently."

"But now you know more?" Vonni asked.

"Some," he said, taking a turn at hedging himself. "We just came across a little more information." His eyebrows pulled together in a half frown.

But he obviously wasn't going to tell her more than that because then he said, "So your grandfather developed the makeup and started his own company with it.…"

"Actually, it was my grandfather's cousin, Phil, who did the business end of things. Phil was a car salesman and he thought that he and Abe could go into the cosmetics business. My grandfather would be in charge of development and production, Phil would do everything else—marketing, sales, delivery. And Hunter Cosmetics was born."

"It was in its infancy when H.J. came on the scene, right?"

"It was in the initial stages of succeeding," Vonni corrected. "And it wasn't only H. J. Camden who came to my grandfather and Phil with their offer. There was someone named Hank, too…"

"My grandfather, H.J.'s only son—Henry James Junior. He was called Hank."

"Ah." Vonni had known the name, not the relationship. But she didn't judge the son to be any better than the father.

Not that there was anything hostile in her tone. Instead, it was neutral, conversational. The same way Dane's was, probably because what they were talking about was so far removed from them both.

"I knew there were two Camdens who met with my grandfather and Phil," Vonni said. "They didn't want to just buy the products for their stores, though, they wanted to buy out Hunter Cosmetics."

"It's something H.J. started and something we've stuck with—if it's more cost-efficient for us to produce what we sell, that's what we like to do."

Vonni wanted his attention to wander, wanted him to start texting someone while he only half listened to her—things that had happened on bad dates—but Dane was still interested. He was participating. Being open and sharing information with her. Providing a good exchange.

Why couldn't you be someone different and have come around months ago?

But he was who he was and it wasn't months ago, so she forced herself to steer away from that dangerous train of thought and focus back on what he was saying.

"But H.J. and my grandfather wanted Abe and Phil to come to work for them," Dane added. "The plan was to have Abe continue to mastermind the cosmetics line, and hire Phil in sales."

"Phil wasn't thrilled with that," Vonni said, repeating the story she'd been told several times growing up. "He'd gone from selling cars to co-owning Hunter Cosmetics. He didn't want to go back to just selling again. And my grandfather didn't want either part of the deal—he didn't want to hand over his formulas to anyone and he didn't want to go to work for Camdens. So they said no to the offer."

"Then H.J. sweetened it. Considerably," Dane filled in, popping a French fry into his mouth.

"That didn't matter to my grandfather," Vonni said. "But the second offer was substantially higher—"

"And at that point Phil liked the idea of all the money he could make selling out," Dane said before taking a drink of his beer. "I guess your grandfather hadn't taken out patents on his formulas...."

"No. He was keeping them as trade secrets, locked in a safe that only he and Phil knew the combination to. When the offer to buy the formulas went up, Phil stole the formulas and sold them to H.J. and Hank. Then he disappeared with all the money."

"Hunter Cosmetics was set up in a way that allowed Phil to make the business deals, right? Even without Abe's say...." Vonni had the sense that Dane was being more careful about what he said .

"It was my grandfather's biggest regret. So the sale was binding and my grandfather had lost his formulas. Phil and the money were nowhere to be found. And H.J. and Hank Camden got what they wanted."

Raising one eyebrow, Vonni gave Dane a challenging look. "But they knew, didn't they? And rather than do the ethical thing—rather than making sure my grandfather was in on the agreement—they turned a blind eye and bought stolen property."

Dane flinched with flourish. "Ouch!"

They were talking academically and there continued to be nothing hostile in Vonni's tone—or in her feelings about something that had happened so long ago. So she smiled and went on, purposely maintaining the challenging look on her face. "The formulas belonged to my grandfather. Phil stole them from him. Your family bought them. Do you see it differently?"

"To be fair, when Phil made the deal, he said Abe had changed his mind." But Dane wasn't defensive enough to sound as if he totally believed the party line.

Vonni pooh-poohed him. "Come on, they had to have know that wasn't true. My grandfather said he'd given them a once and for all no that same day. And Phil had to have shown up in the middle of the night to sell the formulas because my grandfather had locked them in the safe at midnight and when he found it empty first thing the next morning and couldn't reach Phil, he called H. J. Camden. He could only get Hank, and Hank played innocent but he confirmed that they already had the formulas in hand, along with the paperwork that made them property of Camdens. If you believe it went down like that *honestly,* then it's because you *want* to believe it," she accused.

"I'll concede that it wouldn't happen like that today," he said with a somewhat shamed smile. "And that H.J. or my grandfather or somebody should have confirmed the sale with Abe rather than just taking Phil at his word—"

"In the middle of the night," Vonni pointed out again with a facetious laugh.

"But the money was paid out to Hunter Cosmetics, not to Phil personally—"

"A check that no one offered to stop payment on even if there was a chance that Phil hadn't cashed it the minute the banks were open that day."

"Phil claimed that he and Abe would both be coming to work for Camdens after all," Dane said. "And even though Phil and the money were gone, Abe still could have done that."

Vonni laughed once more and shook her head. "There was no way! My grandfather wasn't going to go to work for people who had helped rob him, working on exactly what they'd robbed him of. Would you?"

"No," Dane confirmed.

And since his tone held a certain amount of concession to what Vonni was accusing his family of, she conceded a little, too.

"It wasn't as if my grandfather didn't blame Phil for stealing from him—he did. He knew that was who stuck the knife in his back. But he gave the Camdens credit for twisting it because they bought the formulas they had to know weren't coming to them legitimately. So yes, growing up I did hear the Camden name said like a curse, but it wasn't as bad as what was said about Phil."

"Who was never heard from again? Or was he?"

"No, no one in the family ever heard from him or knew what happened to him."

"And Abe died in 1976?"

"Someone in your family kept track of him?"

"When the new information about H.J. and Hunter Cosmetics came to light recently, GiGi did some research."

"Yes, that's when he died. After open-heart surgery."

"But between 1953 and then, what did he do to make a living?"

"He worked for a company that produced hair products, developing shampoos and conditioners and that kind of thing."

"So he went on."

"To raise his family and have a pretty regular sort of life, sometimes wondering out loud just how rich he might have been if things had been different."

Dane absorbed that shot with a stoic nod of his head. "Well, if you come to work for us we'll see what we can do to make it up to him through his granddaughter."

Vonni laughed again, realizing that it had been fun going back and forth with him, and she had to give him credit for working the conversation back to his job offer. "Oh, you're good."

He grinned, and everything was worth it to get to see that.

"I'm just saying...." He shrugged and her gaze went to broad, broad shoulders hugged impeccably by his dress shirt.

"You're just saying I should do what my grandfather wouldn't—give up a partnership and being my own boss to go to work for Camdens."

"You'd still *be* a boss. To hundreds. With not that many of us over you."

She had a sudden, vivid image of Dane Camden over her, but it was purely physical and inappropriate and she chased it away.

"But in the meantime," he said as he paid the bill that had arrived when they'd finished their burgers, "just keep thinking it over and let's do this wedding for my grandmother."

"*That* I can do," Vonni said.

"Without any hard feelings for what happened before?"

"Without any hard feelings for what happened before," she agreed.

And she meant it.

But as they left the Cherry Cricket and said goodnight with plans to meet again Thursday evening, it occurred to Vonni that she *was* having some softer feelings for Dane Camden that she didn't want to have.

That she shouldn't have.

Softer feelings that she wasn't going to let get the best of her.

Even if she was beginning to understand some of the things she'd heard about him and why so many women in his circle wanted a turn with him.

Whether or not it would get them to the altar.

Chapter Three

"Georgianna Camden is getting married? Now, *that's* a wedding I'll have to show up for!"

The excitement in Chrystal Burke's voice was unmistakable when Vonni told her Thursday afternoon that Georgianna Camden's wedding was the latest job to come their way.

Although Burke's Weddings had been Chrystal's college graduation gift from her father, Chrystal only came into the shop sporadically. For an hour here or an hour there, she dropped in to have Vonni update her on what weddings Vonni was doing and—if the bride or groom were of interest to Chrystal—to hear all the details and dig for dirt. But she never offered to help. The actual work was done by Vonni.

Then, if it was a wedding Chrystal wanted to attend but hadn't already been invited to, Chrystal came to the wedding itself—under the guise of the wedding planner—to basically become one of the guests anyway while Vonni oversaw and coordinated the event and ensured that it went smoothly.

It was the way things had been for the eight years Burke's Weddings had been in business—at least after the first few months when Chrystal had come in every day, from opening to closing, and learned that a job was not her cup of tea.

"And am I understanding right—did you say that you're doing all the planning with *Dane* Camden?" Chrystal asked.

"His grandmother is spending time in Montana with a sick friend and can't do it herself. So yes, you heard right—Dane Camden is acting as go-between, with Mrs. Camden having final say long-distance."

"You know, I never got a turn with him...." Chrystal confided as if the idea titillated her.

Vonni's mother, Elizabeth Hunter, had been the personal assistant to Chrystal's mother, Helene. Since both women had had two-year-old daughters when Elizabeth started the job, Vonni had joined Chrystal in the nursery every day, under the supervision of the nanny.

As a result, Chrystal and Vonni had grown up together, friends on opposite ends of the silver spoon, but friends nonetheless. They'd even gone to the same schools until college. Their relationship was sisterly but they had very, very different personalities.

"But you're married again," Vonni reminded Chrystal with a touch of reprimand in her voice. "Marriage number two—that you swore you were going to make work. So you can't have a turn with him now, either."

"Maybe *I* should do this wedding...." Chrystal suggested.

"What do you mean?" Vonni asked, feeling unusually territorial suddenly.

"You know, I could be there for your meetings with Dane Camden. Go along to check out the church or the reception venue or whatever...."

In other words, Chrystal would be there to flirt while Vonni was trying to do a rush job on the Camden wedding.

Chrystal wasn't malicious or spiteful. She just tended to be flighty and self-centered. And since Vonni knew that about her, she didn't ordinarily take offense to what Chrystal said or did. But for some reason Chrystal taking an interest in spending time with Dane Camden rubbed Vonni wrong.

"You'd still be there, too," Chrystal said, "so it isn't as if I'd be *alone* with him or doing anything I shouldn't. I'd just be...you know, working."

Vonni took a breath and held it to fight the increasing annoyance she felt.

She didn't understand why she felt it, but it was eating her alive.

It wasn't as if she was interested in Dane Camden, she thought as she attempted to sort through her feelings and get them under control. He hadn't been arrogant or conceited or conniving or upper-class smarmy the way she'd expected him to be, the way she'd found too many of the other entitled rich boys she'd learned in adolescence to stay away from. But she still wasn't interested. Even despite the fact that he had a good sense of humor, that he seemed humble and down-to-earth, that he was agreeable and cooperative and accessible. And not at all conceited—because if he was aware of how incredibly handsome he was it didn't show.

But no matter how many positive attributes he had,

Vonni was off the find-a-husband carousel, and even if she wasn't, Dane Camden was absolutely *not* someone she would even think of going after.

So what she was feeling about Chrystal tagging along couldn't have anything to do with the man himself.

It was just the inconvenience, Vonni decided.

Because she did have a job to do. And she was in a huge hurry. Too much of a hurry to be able to afford the distraction Chrystal would cause—*that* was why she so, so, so hated the thought of Chrystal butting in on this.

Banking on the fact that she knew Chrystal well, Vonni decided to call her bluff.

"Maybe you should just do this one yourself," Vonni challenged with an edge she couldn't quite keep from her voice, even though she'd convinced herself there was nothing personal in her feelings. "It's June and I have more weddings on my plate than I can handle already. I only took this one on because—" *not* because Dane Camden was involved or had great hair or the bluest eyes she'd ever seen or the best shoulders "—because it's a *Camden* wedding and I didn't dare turn down something that could be a gold mine for the future. But if you want to start working again—"

Oooh, that had come out a little bitchy.... But Chrystal didn't seem to hear it.

"Oh, I don't want to do the work!" Chrystal said guilelessly.

"And because of time constraints he's scheduled all nights and this weekend," Vonni continued in a more conciliatory tone, still with the goal of making things sound unappealing, but trying to make it seem as if she was only thinking of her friend. "What would you tell Richard about not seeing him from now until after this wedding in order to spend that time with Dane Camden—who I believe Richard hates because two of his old girlfriends left him to date Dane Camden instead, didn't they?"

Chrystal made a horrified face. "Oh, Richard would have a fit! He *does* hate Dane Camden—I forgot about that."

"Plus this has to be done in such a hurry that it's going to be business, business, business—there won't be a minute to spare," Vonni went on bleakly. "And meeting with Dane Camden isn't even a drop in the bucket—he'll be in and out and then there will be orders and paperwork and calls and scheduling and confirmations and all the details that will have to be done without him…"

Chrystal made a face. "I forgot about all of that. And no, I couldn't do nights or this weekend—Richard and I are going to Napa this weekend to see his mother." Chrystal sighed regretfully. "But *Dane* Camden…I've barely gotten to see him across a room at parties. I can't ever get anyone to introduce us—men are afraid if they do, you'll go off with him and leave them behind, and other women just want him to themselves."

Vonni was quick to assure herself that that wasn't what she was doing—even unconsciously—that she was *not* feeling the urge to keep him to herself.

"How is he—up close and personal?" Chrystal asked confidentially, as if to find some appeasement.

"I'm just working with him. We haven't been—and won't be—up close or personal."

"Still, you've *talked* to him—I haven't even done that."

"He's very nice," Vonni conceded. "He has good

manners—old-fashioned good manners—holding the door and ordering for me—"

"You've been out to eat with him?" Chrystal demanded, sounding jealous.

"Just at the Cherry Cricket for a dinner meeting because it was the only time and place we could both fit it in."

"But it was just the two of you and he ordered for you? That sounds like a date."

There was no question in Vonni's mind that last night had been a business meeting, not a date. And she made that clear to Chrystal. All the while not admitting that she *had* still gone away from her time with Dane feeling as if she'd been on a date. With someone she wanted to see again....

"He's pleasant enough company," was all she would admit, however. "And nice looking—better in person than in any pictures I've ever seen of him. But you must know that because you've seen him. Otherwise, he's just another guy."

"And wasted on you right now," Chrystal said in a chastising tone because she didn't agree with Vonni's current course of taking a break from the husband hunt.

"And definitely wasted on me," Vonni agreed.

"You're serious about the no-men thing, aren't you?" Chrystal said disapprovingly.

"Yes, I am," Vonni confirmed.

"You're losing valuable time, you know."

"I've already lost valuable time. Years and years of it. I've been on the husband hunt since college. It's been my second job."

"Still," Chrystal persisted.

Vonni had been over and over this. With Chrystal, and on long-distance phone calls with Vonni's mother in Arizona who was in the blush of new romance with a man she'd met at the retirement community she'd moved into. Neither Chrystal nor Elizabeth liked the idea of Vonni taking a hiatus from the husband hunt, and Vonni was almost as frustrated with defending her decision to them as she was with the husband hunt itself.

It was that frustration that pushed her into a rant. "I've been on every internet dating site, Chrys. I've gone to every dating event I've ever heard of. I've done blind dates, dates with friends who I thought maybe could become more than friends, dates with guys I wasn't attracted to just in case an attraction might develop. I've been on dates with newly divorced men to see if I could snatch them up before someone else did. I've *been there* for a widower so when he finished his grieving I might be the one he turned to for the future. I even paid the eighteen-*hundred*-dollar fee to that private matchmaker and took all of her criticism and all of her advice, and still no husband. Instead, I've invested myself in relationships with go-nowhere, commitment-phobic men and ended up with nothing but lost time, lost money and lost energy."

All the while putting her life on hold.

And that was what she wasn't going to do anymore.

"I'm taking Vonni time," she said to Chrystal, what she'd told both of the naysayers several times. "At least six months of Vonni time."

"I just don't understand that. Vonni time? It just sounds boring. And lonely. What are you actually going to *do?*"

"I'm going to get a dog. I've always wanted a dog, but thought I should wait—husband first, then a dog. Now I'm just going for the dog. I'm going to buy a house to bring that dog home to. I'm going to decorate that house with no one in mind but me. I'm going to take a real vacation to somewhere that isn't a meet-a-man destination or cruise or resort. To somewhere I just want to go for the fun of it—"

"It won't *be* fun if you don't have someone to share it with."

Vonni pointed an accusing finger at her friend. "*That's* the kind of thinking that's kept me putting everything off. And what do I have to show for it? No husband so no dog, no house, no vacation to anywhere worth going, no nothing. I've denied myself what I wanted because fate has denied me a husband. Well, no more! Fate may deny me a husband forever, but *I'm* giving myself the rest."

Chrystal looked at her with pity and shook her head. "We'll find you a husband. I'll talk to Richard—some new lawyers have come into his practice. Maybe one of them is single."

"It doesn't matter if they are!" Vonni nearly shouted. "I don't care. I don't want to know. I don't want to meet them. I can't, Chrystal. I'm tired—*exhausted*—by the husband hunt. It's drained me dry. It's sucked the life out of me. And for now I'm done! I just have to be."

"I think that's dumb. Especially now. You're *thirty*. Every year—every day—you let go by without trying to get a man puts you a day closer to being *forty*. Or fifty. Or sixty. And alone with nothing *but* a dog and a house and some vacation snapshots you had to ask a stranger to take of you."

"Thank you for making it sound awful," Vonni said, laughing because to her the course she'd set for herself for at least the rest of the year didn't feel oppressive, it felt freeing.

"Let's look at it like this," she reasoned with Chrystal. "I'm *only* thirty. I can afford to take six or eight or ten months off the husband hunt to concentrate on my-self, to regroup, to recharge, to reset. Then, when I can face it again, I'll be fresh and maybe instead of attract-ing another man who takes, takes, takes and doesn't give back, another man who doesn't have any intention of ever getting beyond the have-a-good-time stage with any woman, I'll attract the kind of guy who wants the same things I want."

"Or, while you're off getting a house and a dog, the kind of guy who wants the same things you want will have found someone else who wants them, too, and they'll be coming to you to plan *their* wedding."

"I won't let myself think like that," Vonni said with a firm shake of her head. She *needed* this breather. She *needed* to put some things in her life that made her feel as if she actually had a life. She *needed* not to just be in limbo, putting everything off until she found a husband.

"Well you *should* think like that," Chrystal decreed, getting up from the sofa in the office to signal that she was leaving. "But you're right not to hang any hopes on Dane Camden—I've heard he has a no-marriage-ever policy. Although…" Chrystal added as if some-thing had just occurred to her. "If you know that going in and you're not looking for a husband right now any-way, a little rest and respite with Dane Camden might be just the ticket."

Why did that idea inspire a wave of excitement?

"No way," Vonni swore to herself and to Chrystal at once. "A dog, a house, a vacation as soon as there's enough of a lull between weddings for me to get away—besides work, those are the only things getting my at-tention. No men!"

Not even Dane Camden.

"And speaking of work…" Vonni said as Chrystal

headed for the office door. "Getting a Camden wedding is a big deal. And it could lead to more of them since there have been a couple other Camden engagement announcements lately—that seems like something to point out to your dad when we have that meeting he promised me this month to talk about partnership."

In spite of the fact that Burke's Weddings had been Chrystal's graduation gift, it fell under the umbrella corporation that Chrystal's father ran, so he had ultimate say and control.

Vonni had decided against telling either Chrystal or her father about the job offer with Camdens yet.

"I'll tell Daddy."

"And set up the meeting?"

"Maybe. But the new girlfriend is keeping him busy so I don't know...."

"He said June and this is business so it'll be during business hours, not girlfriend hours. And we're starting a new fiscal year July 1, so this is a prime time," Vonni pointed out.

"I'll talk to him," Chrystal said. "And you think about having a rejuvenating fling with Dane Camden so you can give me all the details and I can live vicariously through you!"

"All I want from him is his business," Vonni maintained.

"That's the saddest thing you've ever said," Chrystal countered.

But as Vonni walked her friend out, she refused to let anything about her self-imposed holiday from husband hunting get her down.

Dane Camden arrived at Burke's Weddings at six-thirty Thursday evening and Vonni immediately got to work on a marathon of choosing the basics for his grandmother's wedding—times, locations, colors, decorations, floral arrangements, invitations, seating, menu, napkins, linens and chair covers.

They went on until after eleven o'clock, when Vonni began to talk about whether to opt for lace or satin sashes to tie around the chair covers.

That was when Dane sat back in the white velvet tufted seat he was sitting in, held up his large, powerful-looking hands in surrender, and said, "Okay, okay, uncle! I'm crying uncle! Have some mercy, woman! I need food! I need hard liquor! Maybe I need to hunt wild game or toss around a football or *something* that proves I'm still a man!"

Vonni laughed at him and at the notion that he needed anything to prove that he was more man than he was.

He'd again come with his tie and suit coat already removed, wearing bluish-gray slacks and a barely gray dress shirt with the collar button undone and the sleeves rolled midway up his forearms. Thick, muscular forearms.

And sitting in her elegant, all-white and definitely feminine planning room with the Queen Anne chairs around the ornate antique table, he most certainly did not fit in. In fact, he had the air of a bull in a china shop.

But she got the point.

"Enough for tonight," she said.

"More than enough! It's hot wings and beer time. Come on, let's go. I'm gonna get you out of the glare of all this white before you go blind!"

Vonni laughed again. "I spend every day here and haven't gone blind yet."

"It could happen anytime," he said ominously. "We need to get somewhere dark and dingy on the double!"

"I should organize things here before I leave," Vonni

said, knowing that what she *shouldn't* do was go anywhere with him. Especially when he'd already banned
her from working any more tonight so it couldn't be
considered business.

"Come on.... You wouldn't make me eat alone,
would you? And you can't tell me you haven't put in at
least a fourteen-hour day already."

Sixteen, but who was counting.

It was true—Vonni *was* tired and hungry. So she
blamed that for not having the stamina to fight him.

Plus, she wasn't inclined to say good-night to him
quite yet because even planning his grandmother's
wedding with him for the past several hours had been
fun....

"Somewhere close by?" she asked.

"We'll hit that little place in the basement around
the corner from here—they have local beers on tap."

Vonni knew the place—it was a pub that served a
few comfort-food dishes. It was also a prime spot people went after work. Which was what she'd be doing
with Dane Camden, so it would also not qualify as a
date, she told herself.

"Okay," she agreed. "I *am* hungry, and maybe we
can still talk sashes for the chairs to get just one more
thing done?"

"No! You're relentless," he said as if she were torturing him. But he'd joked around and teased her through
most of the work they'd done, so she recognized when
he wasn't being serious now. She did, however, believe
that he had no intention of talking any more about his
grandmother's wedding tonight.

He stood and grabbed his suit coat. "Lock this white
nightmare up and let's get out of it!"

Vonni shook her head at his incorrigibleness. "Let me get my purse and keys out of the office."

"Hurry or I might swoon."

She laughed at his melodramatics again and went to retrieve her things, glad that she'd worn her most comfortable wedge sandals today because she could easily walk the distance to the pub in them.

In her office she put on the crocheted shrug that went over the yellow dress she had on, took her purse from the desk drawer and resisted the urge to pop into the bathroom to check her hair and makeup. She'd worn her hair pulled back in a clasp at her nape and she didn't think anything had come loose, anyway. And fussing with those things made it seem as if she cared what she looked like for Dane, and she wouldn't let herself.

Instead, she left the office without a clue, merely hoping for the best, and returned to the front of the shop where Dane was waiting for her.

And one glimpse of him after even so short a break somehow caused her to be struck all over again by how terrific looking he was. Tall and lean and strong and so much man that there was no question of his masculinity even if they had been talking all evening about doilies and decorations.

But the power of his presence and how terrific he looked were as inconsequential as her hair and makeup, Vonni silently ruled. And in the hope of stifling the effect he seemed to have on her no matter how hard she tried not to be affected by him, she glanced beyond him at the door he held open for her.

"Go ahead out, I have to set the security system," she advised.

He did, still holding the door for her from the sidewalk while Vonni punched in the code to start the alarm. Then she joined him outside, using her key to lock the door after he'd closed it behind her.

It was a beautiful, balmy summer night, and that was what they talked about on the way to the pub. But it wasn't the only thing Vonni thought about.

Images kept flashing through her mind of him taking her hand as they walked. Or putting his arm around her. As if they were a couple.

It was absurd and it was Chrystal's fault, she decided, for planting the idea of having a fling with the man.

But that wasn't going to happen! It absolutely was *not* going to happen!

Attempting to make sure there was nothing personal going on between them, she walked a few inches farther to the side, away from him.

The pub was half-full when they got there. There was no one to seat them so they took a free booth, sitting across from each other.

Positioned like that, it became impossible for her not to look at him and appreciate all over again how terrifically handsome he was even after what was probably a fourteen-hour day for him.

Then, out of the blue, he said decisively, "Satin ribbons, not lace sashes—the lace would be too froufrou for GiGi. You decide whether they should be green or gray or both to stick with the color scheme. Now don't make me talk about any more of this stuff."

"Deal," she agreed, unable to suppress a smile at his unexpected outburst and the fact that he'd complied with what she'd wanted despite his reluctance.

He was a hard man not to like, she realized then. He was easygoing, upbeat, good-natured, smart, quick, funny, warm and altogether nice and pleasant to be around.

Pleasant to *work* with, she mentally corrected when she realized that she had slipped into doing what she'd done when she was dating—she was cataloging attributes that would have helped her judge whether or not to devote more time to someone she'd just met. To judge whether or not he had husband potential.

But she'd removed herself from the husband hunt. And she already knew Dane Camden did not have husband potential. So there was no reason to be listing his attributes. And she didn't need to be sitting there admiring him any more than she should have been imagining him holding her hand or putting an arm around her on the walk from the shop!

Luckily a waiter came to take their order just then, offering a handy distraction from the mindset she didn't want to be in.

Tonight Dane persuaded her to have a glass of wine to go with her nachos, and he ordered beer and wings. When the waiter brought their drinks moments later, Dane took a long pull of his beer, seemed to relax more and after a replete sigh, he looked her square in the eye and said, "You have a horrible job."

"I do not," she countered with another laugh. "I love my job."

"Is this what you always wanted to do?"

"Be a wedding planner? Well, no, not specifically. But I didn't have any really clear idea of what I wanted to do. My degree is just in business."

"So how did you get into it?"

"The shop was Chrystal Burke's college graduation gift from her father—"

"Chrystal Burke..." he repeated. "The name sounds familiar but I don't think we've ever met."

"She says you haven't. But you do travel in similar circles. Her father—"

"Is Howard Burke—the architect and developer who ran for mayor a couple of years ago?"

"That's him. Chrystal and I grew up together and when he gave her the business, she asked me to work with her."

"*With* her? Not *for* her?"

"With her. We're friends. But Chrystal discovered early on that she doesn't much like to work and since she has a substantial trust fund from her grandmother— plus the support of a husband—she doesn't need to. So Burke's Weddings has basically been me for eight years. Well, me and the four people who also work at the shop as my assistants, and then the waitstaff and valets and security and the other people it takes on the actual day of the wedding, depending on the size of the wedding."

Dane arched his well-shaped eyebrows. "You've been with Burke's Weddings for eight years? How long have you been promised partnership?"

For a lot of those eight years.

But Vonni was embarrassed to say that, so she said, "A while. When the shop proved profitable—"

"I heard it was the number-one place to have a wedding planned. And it was your name I heard along with that recommendation, not Chrystal Burke's."

That embarrassed her, too, so she didn't address it, she merely went on with what she'd been about to say. "Even though the shop was a gift to Chrystal, Mr. Burke—"

"Really owns it and calls the shots," Dane said as if it came as no surprise.

"Right. Not on the day-to-day decisions or the staff or any of the weddings or what I do, but—"

"On the bigger picture."

She confirmed that by not denying it. "Anyway,

when the shop proved profitable and Mr. Burke realized that Chrystal wasn't actually doing anything to bring that about—other than letting her name attract her friends and other people who know her or know *of* her—he started talking about making me a partner—"

"To keep you."

"I suppose," Vonni conceded as their food arrived.

"Because you *are* Burke's Weddings—its only asset."

Vonni shrugged. "There's always someone else who can do your job." She was just repeating what had been said numerous times by her grandfather and by her mother, neither of whom had ever taken their employment for granted—and so Vonni didn't, either.

Something about that made him smile thoughtfully, but he didn't respond. Instead, he offered her a chicken wing.

"I'm not a big fan of those," she said, but reciprocated by telling him he was welcome to share her nachos.

"Just give me one chip with a little of everything on it."

Vonni did, marveling again at how down-to-earth he was. There was an overall sense of familiarity that made it seem as if he felt comfortable with her, and that somehow opened the door to her feeling comfortable with him.

There was no doubt that the man had a way about him.

"And you feel sure the partnership will materialize…." he said then.

"You don't," she challenged in response to his tone.

He shrugged and gently, diplomatically admitted that no, he didn't. "From Howard Burke's perspective it isn't to his advantage. And if you've let him slide by on promises for eight years—"

"Why give me partnership when he can get the same thing from me as an employee," Vonni finished for him.

"I could be wrong," he allowed.

Vonni didn't want to entertain the idea that he could be right, so she changed the subject.

"What about you?" she said. "You said you're the guy who gets the impossible done—what does that translate into in the family business?"

"My official title is senior vice president but none of us take those things seriously—"

"Us?"

"We really are family owned and operated. There are ten Camden grandchildren—me and my three brothers and two sisters, and our four cousins. We're the board of directors and we run the whole shebang, each of us doing pretty much just what suits us—"

"That doesn't sound very organized."

He laughed. "It actually is. Somehow it works out. No matter what comes up, there's always one or another of us willing or able to do it. We all do some project development here and there. We all oversee certain things. We all solve problems. If GiGi says, 'Why doesn't Camdens get into the wedding business,' we put that up for discussion, too, even though she isn't really part of the company. But I'm usually the one called in to get things done when no one else is making headway. If deals are becoming difficult or look impossible, I go in and negotiate or juggle or do whatever it takes—"

"Right or wrong?" Vonni couldn't resist the jibe.

"Nope," he said without skipping a beat. "Not right or wrong. I can't speak for the old days, but now I—we all—make sure that no deal goes down unless everyone is satisfied."

"Even if it means not getting what you want?"

"That's usually where I come in. I don't get ruffled or frustrated or mad too easily, so I guess that makes me the diplomat. But I'm also persistent. If we want an area for a new store and it means displacing small businesses, I work with those small businesses until new and better locations have been found for them, or they can go away with enough buyout money to make them happy. If an area doesn't want one of our stores to come in, I negotiate and work with the cynics until they're happy—or at least appeased. I don't accept excuses, but I can also usually get things accomplished without using a heavy hand. Or being underhanded in any way...."

Vonni took that as an admission that what had happened with her grandfather hadn't been completely aboveboard.

"So you're the *reformed* Camdens," she teased with a bit of an edge.

He laughed. "We might have reformed some of the practices, but *we* didn't need reforming. I can honestly say that not a single thing any of us has done since we've come into the business has been anything to be ashamed of."

"You just inherited the reputation along with the business?"

"Afraid so. But that's part of why we do things the way we do them now—to make sure that reputation isn't deserved."

"Anymore," Vonni contributed.

He shrugged and that drew her gaze to those remarkable shoulders of his. "All I can say is that not only do you have my personal promise that if you come to work for us you'll be treated well and you'll find your association with us beyond reproach, but you can write any kind of protection you want into your contract. We know that with you, in particular, our old reputation works against us and we're willing to do whatever it takes to overcome it so I can have you...."

He grinned at his own turn of phrase.

"So *we* can have you *working* with Camdens," he amended. "See? It's too late to be talking business—I'm putting my foot in my mouth."

Was he thinking about *having* her? Himself?

Oh, it *was* late, and her own mind was wandering dangerously.

Their waiter showed up table side again just then to ask if they wanted anything else. After checking with Vonni, Dane said they were finished and the waiter left the check.

Vonni tried to split it with him but Dane wouldn't hear of it. "I'm keeping you working until eleven at night—the least I can do is buy you nachos. Besides, tomorrow night you're providing dinner."

It wasn't actually dinner she was providing. They were scheduled to spend another evening like they had earlier at her shop. Except tomorrow night there would be an abundance of dishes and cakes for him to taste from the caterers and bakers she'd recommended. So while there would be plenty of food eaten, it wasn't actually a meal.

After he settled the bill and they left the pub, Vonni expected them to part ways—him in one direction to where his car was likely parked at the Camden Building, and her to where hers was parked behind her shop.

But instead he insisted on walking her to her car.

"You know I'm just giving you a hard time when I complain about this whole wedding-planning thing, don't you?" he asked along the way. "It's not my forte, but you do make it painless."

Vonni laughed. "I'm glad to hear it. But to be honest you are in a league of your own—I do usually do most of this with the bride. Even if the grooms come along they don't have to be as hands-on as you are."

And why had *hands-on* come out with the tiniest breath of a seductive sound to it?

Vonni hoped he hadn't heard it but the smile she saw from the corner of her eye told her he had.

She was grateful that he didn't comment, though.

Instead, he said, "I'll run everything by GiGi first thing tomorrow morning, and if she wants anything different than what we've set up tonight I'll let you know. But I went pretty strictly by her guidelines, so there probably won't be a problem."

"Would you call—or have your secretary or assistant or someone—call as soon as you've talked to her just to let me know it's safe to put in the orders? I should do that first thing, too, to get things going."

"GiGi will be up at the crack of dawn, and I'll call her then. What time will you be in in the morning?"

Vonni told him.

"I'll be on the phone to you five minutes after that to let you know what GiGi thought so you can put in the orders without losing any time."

"That would be great," Vonni said, appreciating how accommodating he was.

They'd reached the small employee parking lot behind her shop by then. It wasn't well lit and she was always uneasy being there alone after dark so she also appreciated that he was with her.

And that was the *only* reason she was happy he was there, she told herself firmly when it struck her that even after hours and hours of working with him and sharing a late supper on top of it, she still wasn't eager to say good-night....

"Thanks for the nachos and walking me back here," she said as she unlocked the door of her small black sedan, opened it and stepped behind it to face him again.

"The least I could do," he said in a voice that was slightly deeper than it usually was. For no reason Vonni could fathom.

He was looking at her more intently than usual, too, she realized then. Studying her in a way that caused her to wonder what he was thinking about.

Maybe her hair had come loose after all....

Or worse, maybe she had nacho cheese on her chin....

She rubbed at it nonchalantly but didn't feel anything, and something about that made him smile as if she delighted him.

"You know, originally I wasn't altogether pleased with my grandmother for giving me this job," he confessed. "But now...I'm kind of glad she did."

Vonni laughed at him. "An hour ago you said it was a horrible job."

His smile turned into that grin she liked more than she wanted to.

"That was just the need for food and drink talking." His grin tilted to one side. "But all day today I surprised myself by looking forward to tonight, and I don't see that changing tomorrow."

She refused to admit that she'd spent today watching the clock and willing the time to go faster in anticipation of seeing him again, too. She refused to admit that to herself or to him. Even though it was true.

"I'm not surprised that not too many brides bring

their grooms around to work with you—it might cause a lot of weddings to get called off," he said then.

Vonni laughed wryly at that. "I can honestly say that I've never been the cause of any wedding being called off."

"I can't believe it," he said, still staring at her, giving the impression that he liked what he saw.

"It's true." But there was something about the way he was looking at her that was so warm and flattering that it made her feel as if she actually might have the power to turn the heads of other women's grooms—something she'd never felt before, let alone done.

And suddenly, out of the blue, she wasn't imagining him holding her hand or putting an arm around her the way she had been earlier. She was imagining him kissing her....

Which was totally inappropriate, and she told herself that. She silently shouted it at herself.

But still there she was, looking up into eyes that made her feel beautiful, that made her feel as if no other woman in the world existed. And yes, she was picturing him leaning over that car door and pressing his supple mouth to hers....

Wondering what it would be like....

Wishing he would....

Until she snapped herself out of it again.

Client. He was a client, she shouted in her mind.

And she was on hiatus from men!

And even if neither of those things had been true, she wasn't wasting another minute of her life with a man who wasn't marriage material—and Dane Camden apparently might as well have taken out a billboard announcing that no one was ever getting him to the altar.

So Vonni stood a little straighter, putting just a smidgen more distance between them, forcing herself to think of the door as her shield against him.

"Can I drive you to your car?" she offered, swearing to herself that it was nothing more than she would do for any other client.

"Nah," he said. "I'd better walk off all that blue-cheese dressing I ate with the wings. And you'd better get home—it's late."

Once more fighting the image of him leaning over that door to kiss her, Vonni got behind the wheel of her car and started it. Then she pushed the button to lower the window as he closed the door after her.

"Tomorrow night at six-thirty?" she said to confirm.

"Maybe six-fifteen," he said, as if he might not be able to wait until six-thirty.

"I close the shop at six and that's when the food is due to be delivered. I was just going to get everything ready between six and six-thirty. But you can come anytime after six if you don't mind watching the setup."

"I don't," he said with that secret sort of smile again, hinting that he liked looking at her no matter what she was doing.

"I'll just see you tomorrow night, then. Whenever...."

"Whenever...." he repeated as he stepped away from her car so she could pull out of her spot.

Which Vonni did, spending her short drive home feeling just a little flushed and aglow with the warmth Dane Camden had induced in her.

And understanding more and more why he was the cure so frequently recommended for any woman who needed a boost.

Chapter Four

"**O**rdinarily this process would be spread out—I'd have you sample different caterers on different days, and we'd go to each bakery separately," Vonni explained to Dane on Friday evening. "But because of the rush we're in, we're doing it all here tonight."

He'd arrived at the shop at six o'clock sharp, just when the food was being delivered. Recalling the exchange they'd had at the end of the night before—and the fact that he'd called her himself this morning to give his grandmother's go-ahead and then chatted a little before hanging up—it was tempting for Vonni to believe he'd come earlier than planned because he was eager to be with her again.

But she resisted that temptation and still tried to tell herself that it *was* Friday, he probably hadn't wanted to hang around his office any longer than necessary, which was why he hadn't waited until six-thirty to come to the shop. That it didn't have anything to do with being eager to see her.

But deep down there was a part of her that hoped that was the reason....

She was having the tasting in the same planning room they'd used the night before. As she organized and arranged the food on the antique table that was the size of a conference table, he stood nearby watching and she explained how she thought it best to taste so many things at one sitting.

"I think we should go through course by course, trying what each caterer sent and comparing the dishes. Some might fall short on one course or another, but I'll keep track, and at the end we can see who came out ahead overall. And I wouldn't recommend taking more than a bite or two of each taster—we have hors d'oeuvres, soups, salads, fish, beef and chicken dishes, pastas and sides. Then we have wedding cake—three different bakeries sent four cakes each. That means a dozen kinds of wedding cake to test, too."

"So a bite here, a bite there, will add up," Dane summarized.

"Exactly. One of the caterers sent sorbets as palate cleansers, so that will help, but there'll be that to eat, too. And to drink I can get you soda or iced tea or lemonade, but I'd recommend sparkling water—also to clear the palate."

He pretended disappointment. "What? No wine for every course?"

"Sorry. But I did talk to my liquor people today and I negotiated the champagne you asked for down to two hundred dollars a bottle—"

"That's a bargain price for that champagne," he said, sounding impressed.

"Plus I got a discount on the rest of the liquor for the wedding, too." Which still put the bill for the liquor alone at what many people paid for their entire wedding.

But Vonni didn't point that out. This was a Camden event, the wedding of the matriarch of the entire Camden clan—it might be a relatively small affair, but there weren't any corners being cut.

"You're trying all this stuff, too, aren't you? You wouldn't make me eat alone…."

Ordinarily no, Vonni didn't join her clients in this endeavor, she just took notes. But there wasn't anything ordinary about the way this wedding was being planned. And in envisioning how to do the tasting tonight, and thinking about what she'd already learned about Dane Camden, she'd had a feeling that he wouldn't want to do this while she merely stood by and watched.

So she'd decided to participate.

But not because she was engineering having dinner with him for a third night—she made that point perfectly clear to herself. It was for the client's sake, plus it would give her the opportunity to check up on the caterers she recommended to most of her clients to make sure they were still worth using. So all the way around it was only a matter of business.

"Yes, I'll try everything, too," she assured.

"Great!" he said. "Tell me where the sparkling water is and I'll get us some while you do this."

He was pitching in? That had never happened before. For what Burke's Weddings charged, people expected to be pampered. But again, there was nothing ordinary about this situation. Or maybe about Dane Camden, either….

Vonni considered declining his offer, but she liked

that unaffected part of him too much to squelch it, so she told him where to find the water and let him get it.

By the time he returned, Vonni had everything ready to go.

"Appetizers," she announced as they sat in their respective seats—Dane at the head of the table and Vonni next to him on his right.

She explained what each offering was and then they tasted them, with Vonni taking only tiny bites because she knew she wouldn't be able to make it to the end if she didn't, and writing down Dane's likes and dislikes as they went along.

They might not have agreed on chicken wings the night before, but other than that, Vonni had to admire his choices. There was nothing he liked that she didn't, nothing he disliked that she didn't agree with, and for all the same reasons.

Along with eating, she also showed him portfolios from the photographers she recommended. Not only did that get something else accomplished, but it also allowed them some much-needed pauses in all the tasting. And left Vonni approving of his eye for photography as much as his palate.

There were just so many sides to the man. And she hadn't found one yet that was bad....

They took the longest break before they started on the cakes, assessing the caterers and deciding which one to use and what menu to go with.

Then they moved on, making quicker work of the cake tasting before Dane texted his grandmother his recommendations, including a four-tier cake with chocolate on the bottom, carrot on the second tier, and white for both of the top two, all covered in silver-gray fondant and adorned with green fondant vines and multi-colored flowers.

When his grandmother texted back her approval of everything, Dane held up his hands as if he were crossing a finish line and said, "Done! For tonight, anyway."

"I'll call everyone tomorrow morning to let them know," Vonni said.

But despite the fact that they were finished, he showed no signs of leaving. Instead, he sat back in his chair, rested an arm on the table and said, "I keep wondering about something you said last night—that you and Chrystal Burke are friends—"

"We are."

"But I at least know *of* Chrystal Burke even though we haven't formally met. So if she and I run in similar circles—the way you said last night—then you must, too. And how could I possibly have missed you? Believe me, you are not overlookable…."

The flattery caused Vonni to smile involuntarily. "Chrystal and I are friends—we grew up together. But we haven't *ever* run in the same circles," she said.

"How does that work?" he asked, confused.

"My mom was Chrystal's mother's personal assistant. She started that when I was two and since Chrystal was also two, I sort of came along as a package deal to be Chrystal's playmate."

"So you went to work with Mom every day at the Burkes' house?"

"Right. That way my parents didn't have to pay for day care, my mom was always close by and I had the advantages of the Burkes' nursery and nanny."

"And when it was time for school?"

"The Burkes' influence helped get me scholarships to the same private schools Chrystal went to—all the way from preschool through high school. So Mom could bring me along to work with her in the morning, the Burkes' driver would take us to school and pick us up afterward and I'd go back to the Burkes' until Mom was done for the day."

"And college?"

"For college I got my own scholarship on merit, but it was for the Denver campus of the University of Colorado, and Chrystal went to Denver University, so that was the first time we parted ways. But by then my mother and I were living in a cottage on the Burkes' estate, and Chrystal just commuted for classes every day to DU, so we were still close."

"Just not running-in-the-same-circles close?"

"She ran in the Haves circles, I ran in the Have-nots circles," Vonni said simply enough.

"So you and Chrystal Burke were friends at home, but she snubbed you at school?"

"She didn't snub me. She just had her friends and I had mine—the way sisters do, I guess."

"Were you okay with that?" he asked as if he was reserving judgment on Chrystal until he heard the answer.

"I actually was," Vonni assured him. "I think the world of Chrystal. But when it came to my other friends I liked the more—" she didn't want to say anything that might insult him so she chose her words carefully "—the more straightforward, unaffected kids—"

Although as she said the words, she realized that they seemed to apply to him, too. And that was why it was becoming increasingly difficult not to like him. He wasn't pretentious or snobby, he wasn't full of himself, he wasn't any of the things that were so pervasive among Chrystal's crowd. Any of the things that could so naturally have come from being who he was.

"My friends were the other scholarship kids," she went on. "The practical kids. The kids who *had* to be practical the way I did. I never wanted to put on airs or pretend I was something I wasn't. Or that I had things I didn't have. With my friends, I didn't need to."

"Okay, but you can't tell me that—looking the way you do—every guy in every school, including the *Haves,* didn't want to...*fraternize* with you."

Flattering again. And again Vonni couldn't help smiling. She appreciated that he thought that.

"I, uh…" How to say this part without offending him? "I wasn't very trusting of the Have guys. There were too many times when one of my friends let herself be swept off her feet by one of them and got burned. We were okay to...mess around with, but in the end we weren't who they were going to bring home. I knew that no one wanted to take me to the country club and introduce me as the daughter of Mrs. Burke's assistant."

"You must have known some pretty shallow guys."

Vonni shrugged, not wanting to get into the subject, since Dane might have fit that description in the past even if he didn't seem to now.

"Were you happy to go to the private schools or would you have rather gone to public school?"

"I never went to public school so I don't know the difference. But I loved school," she said. "The way I loved going to the Burkes' with my mom every day before that. Until my dad died they were both places that were… I don't know, so much calmer and more controlled than home was, I guess."

Dane frowned. "There were problems at home?"

"There were problems between my parents. They both loved me and I knew that, but they were not what you would call happily married. In fact, sometimes I thought they hated each other."

"For any particular reason…?"

"Like cheating or gambling or drinking or something? No. I think they just grew not to like each other. They married right out of high school—they were only kids. If they had met when they were adults, they probably wouldn't have gone out on a second date—they didn't like to do the same things, they didn't have the same interests, they didn't see eye to eye on anything. But by the time they were their adult selves and discovered they were so different from each other, they were married and had me."

"No more than you?"

"Nope, just me. And it was one of those stay-together-for-the-kid things. Where the kid wished they wouldn't…." That wasn't something she told too many people.

Dane laughed kindly. "You *wanted* your parents to get divorced?"

"I sort of did. They fought night and day, about everything, big and small."

"In front of you?"

"That isn't ever where it started, no—they put effort into keeping it under wraps. But it would go on and on and get so heated that eventually they couldn't hide it."

"That does not sound like a good way for anybody to live," Dane commiserated. "For them or for you—no wonder you were happy to go to school. And then your dad died?" he asked carefully.

Vonni laughed wryly at the caution in his tone. "My mother didn't kill my father, if that's what you're thinking."

"It crossed my mind," he admitted.

"But actually the fighting and my father's own anger did," she added sadly. "He stormed out of the house during one of their screaming matches—it was something he did pretty often. I was watching from my bedroom window and he nearly hit the tree across the street from our house because he just gunned the ignition backing up. The tires were screeching when he drove off and about an hour later the police showed up. He'd been driving really, really fast—they'd calculated his speed at over eighty miles an hour. He'd blown through a stop sign at the bottom of a steep hill, lost control of the car and rolled it. Luckily he hadn't hit anyone else, so he was the only casualty, but he died at the scene."

"I'm so sorry. How old were you?"

"Twelve. In the end I guess they were married till death did them part in the worst way," Vonni said sadly.

"And now you're a wedding planner—there's some irony in that."

"I know," Vonni answered with another dry laugh. "Maybe I'm trying to make happy marriages to compensate. Or prove to myself that they can exist. I know I had friends whose parents were happily married and I guess maybe I still wanted—want—to believe it's possible for two people to find each other, make a life together, build on that and live happily ever after."

"I think it's possible. Anything is possible," Dane said. But it sounded as if it was purely academic to him.

"It just isn't something you're looking for yourself," Vonni pointed out. "Not now. Not ever. Never," she said, repeating what he'd told her when they'd first met and she'd assumed the wedding he was hiring her to plan was his own.

"Right," he confirmed simply.

"Well, at least you're honest," Vonni said with a genuine laugh, thinking that she wouldn't have wasted as much time as she had if some of the men she'd dated had been as direct.

"Anyway," she said, getting back to the subject of her friendship with Chrystal. "After my dad died, Mrs. Burke offered a cottage on the Burkes' estate for my mom and me to live in. So even though Chrystal and I had different groups of friends, we really did grow up like sisters from the time we were both two all the way through college. I was the wedding planner *and* the maid of honor for her first wedding, but no, I don't get invited to the parties or the charity events she gets invited to. I don't belong to her country club, and her friends still aren't my friends."

"So the odds that you and I have been at the same place at the same time are slim," he finished for her. "And it isn't that I've overlooked the unoverlookable."

"*Unoverlookable*—should I add that to my dating profiles?" she joked.

He laughed. "You say that as if you have a lot of those."

Whoops. She was aware that she'd already done more talking about herself than she probably should have—the man just seemed to draw her out and he *was* an extremely good listener. But she didn't have any intention of telling him about her husband-hunting past on top of it.

"Oh, yeah, I have dozens of dating profiles," she answered so facetiously it sounded as if it was a lie.

"Well, by all means add *unoverlookable*. Because you are." He was watching her intently and his expression said that he was enjoying the view. Then, in a more intimate tone, he said, "And I'm reasonably sure that if I'd ever run into you before I would have remembered. You're unoverlookable, noteworthy and unforgettable...."

Vonni laughed in embarrassment at the accolades and felt the need to make light of it. "Uh-huh, that's me, all right. Everyone says so."

"They should because it's true," he said sincerely. Then his ruminative smile became a grin and he said, "And you blush nicely, too—I don't run into that much in my *circles*...."

Vonni felt the heat in her face but hoped it wasn't showing. "Maybe I'm allergic to something we ate."

He laughed an appreciative laugh, and that just added to her flush. Plus it didn't help that Dane's eyes remained on her, studying her as if he were cataloging what he liked. All she could think to do was get back to business.

"So..." she said in a more professional tone. "I need to have a look at the house where the wedding reception is being held to get an idea of the layout, where it's best to set tables and chairs, what will work for the flow of things. It'll be at your grandmother's house, right?"

"Right. Where *I* grew up," he answered with some amusement in his tone that told her he knew she was using the change of subject as a dodge. But he cooperated anyway and said, "How about tomorrow?"

"The sooner the better," Vonni told him. "But I have overlapping weddings tomorrow—one at eleven in the morning and another, much bigger one at two that will keep me busy until at least seven tomorrow night—"

"I told you I was at your disposal, so whatever works for you—we can do it after the second wedding tomorrow night."

"Could we do it at eight—just to be safe?" she asked as if she were stretching a boundary.

"Sure," he answered without hesitation.

"At least with your grandmother out of town it shouldn't disturb anyone."

"Actually, Margaret and Louie are there but they won't mind. I'll call and warn them we're coming."

"More family?"

"Family, yes, but not related. Margaret and Louie Haliburton. They live there and take care of the place inside and out, but they've worked for GiGi for so long they've become her best friends, and we all consider them family. So much so that rather than play favorites by choosing among the grandchildren, GiGi asked Margaret to be her matron of honor, and Louie is giving the bride away—that's how close they are."

"That's nice," Vonni said, but at the same time thinking that Mrs. Burke would never have included Vonni's mother that way, and about the fight Chrystal had had with her parents to have Vonni as Chrystal's attendant at her first wedding. They'd considered it unseemly regardless of how close Chrystal and Vonni were.

"So if you have a morning wedding, you probably want to get home," Dane said, sounding guilty. "I shouldn't have kept you here talking."

"It was me *doing* all the talking," she pointed out.

"At least let me help you clean up and I'll walk you out to your car so you don't have to go into that dark parking lot by yourself."

She wished she could take him up on his thoughtful offer. But she couldn't.

"Thanks, but I have more work to do tonight before I can head home. Two weddings means two sets of last-minute details to check on."

"Is there anything I can do to help? How about if I clean this up while you handle your *details?*"

Vonni appreciated his consideration but she couldn't let her client—a Camden—essentially act like her janitor.

"Absolutely not. I'll probably let this all wait until morning, and just get to the other things I need to accomplish before I can go home," she lied, having every intention of not leaving tonight until the place was clean.

"You're sure there's nothing I can do? I *am* the one who heaped another wedding on you when you're already booked…."

"No, honestly. But thanks, anyway."

He stood then—tall and lean and broad-shouldered, looking too good in his casual-Friday khakis and buttercream-colored shirt to say good-night to.

Which was all the more reason to do it, she told herself as she walked him to the front of the shop and unlocked the door to let him out.

"I'll text you GiGi's address and the directions to the house," he said as Vonni opened the door and leaned against it to hold it for him. "I'll be there to meet you, but don't worry if something happens and you can't make it right at eight. I'll wait."

"I'll let you know if I'm going to be any later."

"And how about dinner? I could order something in or we could go somewhere when you're finished checking out the place—I want to feed you since I'm extending your day."

"My caterers usually provide the staff with food to keep us all going—not what's being served at the wedding, but sandwiches and things. So I'll probably have eaten."

He nodded and for no reason Vonni could understand it hit her all over again how strikingly handsome he was.

"Okay, then…" He seemed to be stalling as he studied her once more with those intensely blue eyes. "Try not to work too hard tomorrow...."

"Tomorrow is what all the work is for, and I'll just be orchestrating and overseeing," she said, not sure if she was making sense.

Because suddenly she was really only thinking about Dane and the pure magnetism he exuded.

And how truly fabulous his lips were.

Suddenly she was really only wondering if he was as good with them as she'd heard....

No, no, no! Not the kissing thoughts again!

She tried to curb them but he was standing very close in front of her, looking down at her with those deep blue eyes, and they were just so...in position....

Then he reached a hand to her upper arm, to the skin left bare by the cap sleeves of her white summer shirtwaist dress.

And he used that hand—big and warm and strong— to give her a little squeeze....

She told herself it was only a friendly gesture. They were spending a lot of time together, getting to know a little about each other. Being friendly, that was all.

But she already had kissing on the brain so she half expected him to pull her toward him.

And half expecting it, she found herself tilting her chin upward invitingly....

Until she realized what she was doing and pulled back.

No kissing! she commanded herself.

And there wasn't any.

Because a moment after that, Dane gave her arm a second squeeze and took his hand away as he told her he hoped everything went well for her the next day. Then he said good-night.

"'Night," Vonni said after him.

But as she locked the door behind him and replayed the past few moments in slow motion in her mind, she realized that he just might have leaned toward her a little, too.

Chapter Five

"This is a beautiful house," Vonni said when she entered the Camden family home a little before eight o'clock on Saturday night. "It's amazing from the outside and inside it's warm and comfortable and inviting—you don't always find that with houses this size." She liked it much more than the places she'd had occasion to visit in meeting with other clients.

"It's all GiGi," Dane said as he showed her into the foyer of the enormous Tudor mansion.

The foyer had a high vaulted ceiling with a crystal chandelier centered over a large round entry table. Dane introduced the older man and woman standing near it as Margaret and Louie Haliburton. After exchanging convivial small talk, they left—with a reminder from Margaret that there was a plate of cookies for them in the kitchen.

"How are you holding up?" Dane asked when they were alone.

It wasn't a question she heard from clients and he asked it with genuine interest and consideration—all things that felt good to come home to.

Not that she was coming home to him. But for some reason he made it seem as if she was. And it felt good. It just felt good to be with him again—something she'd wanted since he'd left her shop the night before.

But she couldn't let herself consider the implications of that. Especially not when she'd sworn to herself on the way over that she was not going to let tonight go the way previous evenings had—she was going to keep this visit strictly professional, go in, do what she'd come for and go home. Without thinking about kissing the client. Or imagining that he might be on the verge of kissing her.

"I'm holding up okay," she answered. "Both weddings went as planned, without any glitches—"

"I heard you're known for your glitch-free weddings— I figure you can set up a training program for Camden wedding planners so they'll learn your tricks."

Vonni chose to ignore that. "So besides being a long day, it was fine."

"But it *was* a long day," he persisted. "If you want to kick off your shoes and walk barefoot around here, I won't tell."

Vonni laughed. She was tempted. But in keeping with her determination to make this quick and professional, she declined. "Thanks, but the feet are doing okay."

He bent over slightly to look down at the strappy wedges she'd chosen specifically because she could be in them for hours without a problem.

Then his eyes went slowly—and appreciatively—up her nylon-encased legs to her dress. It was one of the many she specifically wore on a wedding day—a navy blue, knee-length sheath with a boat neck.

"You certainly don't look like you've been working all day and most of tonight."

"That's the goal, so thank you," she said.

She'd removed the matching jacket, but her outfit was still work attire, and she envied Dane his more casual gray golf pants and yellow polo shirt.

She also noticed how the shirt accentuated his broad chest and shoulders, but she tried to ignore it.

"Margaret was baking the cookies when I got here," he said. "We can dig into those when we're finished looking around and really put your workday behind you."

Vonni thought she'd smelled fresh baking when she'd come in the door. "I'm a sucker for chocolate-chip cookies," she said, knowing even as she did that she was going against her vow to do this quickly and leave. But how long could it take to eat just one cookie?

"Let's get this over with, then, so we can relax," he suggested. "The den is over there." He motioned to the right of the entranceway. "That's where the ceremony itself will be—GiGi and Jonah are having a judge do that part without fanfare. While it's going on, you and the caterers and whoever else on your staff can be working out here—we'll close the doors to the den and you can have free run of the place."

The double doors to the den were open now and Vonni glanced through them at the stately oak-paneled room. But because she didn't have anything to do with that portion of the event, she had no reason to poke her nose into it and didn't.

"Can we use this table for the guest registry and gifts?" she asked, nodding at the entry table. "I'll cover it with a cloth to protect it, but the positioning and size are perfect. Unless you don't want it used, and then we can move it somewhere else and set up another table for the gifts and a podium for the registry. Or…" she said, looking at the wide curving staircase with its carved oak posts and banister rising to the second floor, "we could put gifts along the side of the stairs—by the way, do you want them blocked off so guests only have access to this floor?"

"It's just going to be friends and family so I don't think we have to worry about anybody wandering. And as for the table, this is a user-friendly place—it's had to be—so the table can stay *and* be used."

He pointed to the left where a wide passageway led to a formal living room. "They want the reception to be on the patio, but there's no way back there from outside—"

"Is there a rear entrance for the caterers to use?"

"No, that was turned into an entrance from the house to GiGi's greenhouse a long time ago. They'll have to come in the front and so will the guests. The caterers can go straight back to the kitchen from here—" he pointed to a corridor that ran the length of the staircase "—but the guests are going to have to pass either through the kitchen or go through the living room and out the dining room doors to get to the patio. And I don't think we want them going through the kitchen."

"No, the caterers will be in there and foot traffic would be bad. But before we get to that, let's talk about parking," Vonni said.

She'd taken note of the arrival-and-departure situation when she'd driven up the stone-paved drive that circled a large fountain and passed in front of the five-car garage. "I think you're going to need to hire valets to park cars. Not too many more than the family's cars are going to fit out front."

He agreed with that and she assured him she had licensed and bonded people she used.

Then she asked him to show her the path he wanted the guests to take through the spacious and elegant living and dining rooms to get to the four sets of French doors that opened to the outside. Along the way they discussed several carpet-saving possibilities and Vonni assured him she would make it elegant.

From there they went out onto a tiled patio that was partially covered and provided a full outdoor kitchen complete with sink and running water. There was more than enough space to accommodate tables and chairs for a hundred people as well as a dance floor, and they needed only to discuss where to set everything up and whether or not to erect a tent in the area that wasn't covered.

Before all the decisions were made the sun went down, allowing Vonni to see the lighting that would be available. That was when she suggested that rather than a tent, they put up a canopy of white lights on wires strung from the house to the forest of oak trees that surrounded the patio.

"It will give a lot of extra light and look beautiful against the sky and the overhang of the tree branches," she told him.

Dane agreed, and after going through her checklist to make sure she had all she needed, Vonni said, "I think that's everything."

"Now we can eat cookies—they're just waiting for us in the kitchen."

"Actually that's perfect because I need to check the

kitchen so I can let the caterers know what kind of area they'll have to work in."

"And *then* we'll be done...." he said with feigned exasperation, as if he'd reached his limit on wedding talk. He ushered her back inside, this time through a set of sliding doors that led directly into the kitchen.

It was restaurant size but as warm and homey as the rest of the place. Navy-blue-and-white tile formed a checkered pattern in the floor, there were tarnished brass lighting and plumbing fixtures, pristine white cupboards, a commercial-size refrigerator, a six-burner gas stove, built-in grill, double ovens, three sinks, an expansive island in the center of the room for ample workspace and a breakfast nook large enough to be a conference table.

"Oh, there's no problem in here, either," she said with relief after just one glance around. "The caterers are going to be thrilled—there's plenty of room to work and more than enough surfaces for trays and platters and food."

"Great! Now are we done?" Dane asked.

Vonni made a few more notes for the caterers then said, "Okay. Done!"

Dane snatched her binder out of her hands and set it where she couldn't reach it on top of the enormous refrigerator.

"Don't let me leave without that!" she said fearfully.

"Leave your pen on the counter as a reminder so we can have cookies in peace."

One cookie and she should go—that was what Vonni had told herself.

But it had been a terribly long day and the kitchen still smelled of freshly baked cookies and she just couldn't make herself turn him down when he pulled out a bar stool and ordered her to sit.

"We could go the tried-and-true route of milk with the cookies," he said then. "But there's a nice little dessert wine GiGi has that's especially for chocolate—what do you say we do this that way?"

"Cookies and wine instead of cookies and milk?" Vonni repeated as if she needed to think it through. But she wasn't much of a milk drinker so what she was really doing was trying once again to talk herself into taking one cookie and leaving.

It didn't work this time, either. Not when she factored in that it *was* Saturday night and she *had* just worked until after nine o'clock, and being with him somehow seemed to naturally relax her to such a degree that she wanted to wind down the rest of the way, too.

"Okay, I'm game," she heard herself say, even as a voice in the back of her mind told her she shouldn't.

"Wine it is!" Dane said, grabbing a bottle from the counter beside the refrigerator as if he'd known all along he would be able to persuade her and had set it there just for the taking.

But rather than giving that too much thought, Vonni glanced through the windows of the breakfast nook toward the patio in the distance. "This is a beautiful place for a wedding—no wonder your grandmother didn't want to have it anywhere else."

"They really just wanted it to be at home," he answered as he poured the wine.

Then he brought the two glasses to the island and sat on a bar stool adjacent to her. "Shoes off, hair down now?" he said like the spider to the fly, making her laugh.

It *was* tempting to kick off her shoes and take her

hair out of the French twist it was in. But she couldn't go that far. "I'm fine," she insisted, taking a cookie from the plate he held out to her.

He gave her a napkin, then took a napkin and cookie for himself.

"These are one of Margaret's specialties. She says she uses three different kinds of chocolate chips so there are levels of chocolate, and she toasts the nuts—whatever that means—before she puts them in. Pecans, I think," he informed her.

"Ooh…they are fantastic!" Vonni judged after taking a bite.

"Now sip the wine—that's how you get the full effect, I'm told."

They both tasted their wine and agreed that the combination was surprisingly complementary.

"Wine and cookies—I would have never thought of that," Vonni said.

"My cousin Cade discovered the wine at a wine tasting he went to with our groom's granddaughter—and now Cade's fiancée—Nati Morrison. You'll meet them all at the wedding."

Vonni laughed again. "I'm not usually introduced to the guests. I'm a behind-the-scenes person."

"Maybe not so much for this one—we all want you to run Camden's wedding departments, so everybody is interested in who you are and will want to meet you."

Not only would she be working, she would be on display and on a job interview for a position she still wasn't really considering? That was more than she wanted to think about at the moment, so she changed the subject.

"You always refer to this as your grandmother's house," she said. "But you mentioned last night that this is where you grew up?"

"From when I was nine. That was when my parents, my aunt and uncle and my grandfather were killed in a plane crash."

She hadn't meant to get into a subject quite that dark. "I'm sorry. I knew there was some tragedy a long time ago in the Camden family but I didn't know what it was—"

"It *was* a long time ago," he said, dismissing her concern. "But that's when I came to live here. With my three younger brothers, my younger sisters Lindie and Livi—who, along with Lang, are triplets—and our four cousins. You met Jani, and there's Seth, Cade and Beau, too."

"*Ten* kids came to live here all at once, without any parents?"

"And GiGi raised all of us," he confirmed. "With the help of H.J.—who had to come out of retirement at eighty-eight to run the business again—and Margaret and Louie."

"I can't imagine…."

He laughed. "As an only child, no, I don't suppose you can."

"Ten kids all in one house…."

"The place is looking a little smaller to you now, isn't it?"

"I can't even picture what that might be like."

"Never-ending summer camp or boarding school— a whole lot of chaos and commotion and noise and activity and work."

"Did you like it or not?" she asked when they both started on their second cookie. She couldn't tell from his tone.

"It was the way things were," he said with a shrug. "At first it wasn't so great. We'd lost our parents and

grandfather and aunt and uncle—so there was grieving and what that brings with it in kids. And we'd had
to leave our homes—we all liked visiting GiGi and
Gramps, but now we had to *live* here. None of that was
easy on anybody. But once we all got over the hump,
it just was what it was—a great big family with GiGi
at the head of it—"

"Not H.J.?"

"He was eighty-eight," Dane repeated. "He was
doing his best to keep the business going and set it up
to be maintained until we were all old enough to take it
over—which he did with a board of directors he hand-
picked and trusted in case he didn't live long enough
to hang on to the reins himself."

"Did he?"

"He lived to be ninety-six, but the oldest of us—my
cousin Seth—was only nineteen then, so no, there was
a period of time when the board of directors ran things
with GiGi overseeing them, too, to make sure nothing
went wrong. We all took over little by little as each of
us graduated from college—we were mentored by the
members of the board until the ten of us could do it on
our own. But around here, GiGi was the undisputed
head of the family. She ran the household, with H.J.,
Margaret and Louie her support team, and older kids
delegated to take care of younger kids, too."

"And you're where in the age range?"

"Top three of the heap—Seth is the eldest, Cade and
I are the same age and just two years behind him. Of
course the rest only drop down in age about a year at
a time, but when there are so many to wrangle, Seth
and Cade and me had to look after the seven younger
kids a lot."

He spoke unemotionally, leaving Vonni wondering

how he felt about that arrangement. "Did you resent being one of your grandmother's delegates?"

"You know…sometimes. I was a kid. At home, before the plane crash, we'd had a nanny who had been responsible for us all, so even though I was the oldest kid on that side I hadn't had to do anything with my younger brothers and sisters—"

"There weren't any nannies when you came here?"

"Nope. GiGi didn't like the idea of nannies. She's from a small town in Montana where 'family takes care of its own'—that's what she's always said. Where the oldest looked after the youngest. And that was how she wanted it here. I don't know if it was part of her plan to make us all close—to make us all feel like brothers and sisters rather than cousins—but it accomplished that. I don't feel any different about any of my cousins than I do about my own brothers and sisters. We really are all just one great big family."

He said that proudly, fondly.

"So it wasn't bad," Vonni said over her third cookie.

"After the initial stuff, no. There was always somebody to kick the football with or play hoops. No game of any kind was ever undermanned. There was always backup if we had problems at school. There was a lot of work, but there were a lot of advantages, too."

Advantages Vonni had missed and longed for as an only child. Which she had no doubt was a contributing factor to her own determination to find a husband and have a family of her own.

But if Dane found family life to be a good thing, why was he so opposed to having one of his own?

"So you like your family and you're close to them all, but when it comes to your own life—"

He grinned. "Yeah… It's not what I want."

"Why is that?" Vonni asked, not quite sure why she felt as if she could.

But Dane didn't balk; he merely answered her question. "H.J. was a titan of business. A giant. A lion at work. At home, GiGi called the shots and he did whatever she said. Margaret says jump, Louie asks her how high. I don't want to become somebody who went from doing what I was told as a kid to doing what I'm told as a husband."

"That doesn't always happen," Vonni argued. "Marriages can be equal—"

"There still has to be give-and-take, and growing up I did more than my fair share of conceding to get by. Now if I want a TV in the bedroom, I don't want to go without a TV in the bedroom because the wife won't hear of it. It's a trade-off. I've already lived by committee. I work by committee. At home I like *not* living by committee and just doing as I please."

"And kids?"

"I feel like I've already done the parenting thing. Or at least enough of it. GiGi wanted us to be close, and part of that was that no one was ever in any sporting event, any play, any concert, any program or graduation without every single one of us being in the audience. I've taught younger siblings and cousins to drive. I've helped with college applications. I've sat up nights to comfort broken hearts or advise on fights with friends. It just seems like I've done the family thing through and through, and now—"

"You don't want to do it again."

"I'm still doing it," he said with a wry laugh. "Sunday dinner every week. Upcoming engagement parties and weddings. And now there'll be Camden tiny tots— once that starts it's bound to avalanche and there will be a birthday party every other minute and Christmas concerts and plays and…there will be a ton more Camdens to have family life with and enough is enough! I'll pass on more work and responsibility and just be Fun Uncle Dane—"

"Fun Uncle Dane," Vonni repeated with a laugh.

"Who can enjoy the good times then go home to my quiet place, breathe a sigh of relief and do whatever I please. It seems like the best of all worlds to me."

"You want to have a family, but once removed, at a distance, where you can keep your hands clean," she teased him.

He laughed. "Yeah. What's wrong with that?"

Vonni pondered it for a moment then took a turn at shrugging herself. "I guess there isn't anything wrong with it if that's what you want. It's just…unusual."

"It's unusual to grow up the way I did, too, looking after seven other kids."

"True. Although my best friend all through school—"

"Besides Chrystal Burke?"

"Right. Anyway, Trudy had four younger brothers and cash-strapped parents who had to work all the time, so she took care of the house and the family as if she was the parent. But she still grew up and wanted a husband and kids of her own. So not everyone burns out on it."

"I don't know if it's so much burnout as been there done that, just don't want to do it again."

Which once more brought home to Vonni how this man wasn't for her at all. They couldn't have more different goals.

So why, even at a moment when it couldn't have been clearer to her that she shouldn't be, was she still attracted to him—because yes, as much as she kept denying it, as much as she didn't want it to be true, she *was* attracted to him. Overwhelmingly attracted to him....

"I should get home," she announced, unsure if she was being rude cutting him off in the middle of a conversation but knowing that she had to get out of there. That she was finally doing what she should have done instead of giving in to her own inclination to spend as much time as possible with him.

"Yeah, I'm sure you're ready to throw in the towel on a workday this long," he said, not sounding put out by her abruptness but definitely seeming sorry that she was leaving.

He got up from his bar stool and retrieved her binder from the top of the refrigerator.

Vonni's initial response was merely to watch him, to revel in the sight of his lean, well-muscled body moving across the space, reaching a long, powerful-looking arm to the towering fridge.

Then she caught herself and stood, too, just as he turned to hand her the binder.

"I'll walk you out to your car and then come back in here and lock up," he said.

"You don't have to do that. I'm right out front."

"Come on," he said, refusing to argue. "Let's get you home so you can rest, and you can tell me what's on the agenda for tomorrow."

"You said you have Sunday dinner every week...." she reminded him as they headed out of the kitchen through the corridor that the caterers would use. "Tomorrow was the day for shopping for the welcome gift baskets and what to put in them for your out-of-town guests, but I can do that on my own if you need to be somewhere else."

He opened the oversize, arched front door and waited for her to go out onto the landing before following her.

"We do have Sunday dinner here every week, the lot of us with GiGi, Margaret and Louie. But since GiGi is in Northbridge, we're skipping this week. So I'm at your disposal—we can shop for basket stuff all day. Or, if there's more that we can get done, let's do that, too."

And then she could have the entire day with him rather than only part of it.…

Except then she'd be violating the rules she'd set for herself during this break from husband hunting—she'd be putting her own needs on hold for a man.

"I only have you scheduled for half the day—I was going to leave it up to you which half," she said, forcing herself to stick to her original plan. "But either before or after we shop I have some prospective houses to look at because I'm in the market for one, and I need to visit my dog at the shelter."

They'd reached her car by then and Vonni leaned against the hood to rest feet that were beginning to tire, while Dane stood directly in front of her. In the glow of the many lights that lit the front grounds of the Camden house she saw his straight brow furrow a bit.

"Are you between places to live and keeping your dog at the shelter in the meantime?" he asked, confused.

"No, I'm not between places to live—I have a small apartment just outside the city. I just can't have a pet there. I decided to buy a house and then I was going to get myself a dog. It's just that I found the dog before the house."

"An easier acquisition."

"Right. I've always donated what I could and helped out at one of the shelters, and a dog came in that I just clicked with. So, since they know me there, they're doing something they don't ordinarily do—they're letting me board my dog with them until I find a house. But on Sundays I try to get there no matter what."

"You're taking half a day off tomorrow—that's what you're telling me. And I'm glad to hear it—nobody should work as many hours as you do."

He looked into the distance as if he was considering something, then said, "You know...I was wondering what to do with myself without the weekly family dinner to go to tomorrow, and we'll be together to do the shopping, and I like dogs.... What if we work and then I tag along on your Sunday errands? Would I be butting in? Would you hate it? Would that be bad?"

Oh, sooo bad....

Because all he had to do was suggest it, and it was exactly what Vonni wanted.

With another go-nowhere guy, she lamented.

But then she reminded herself firmly that she wasn't looking to go anywhere with any guy right now. So having Dane along on her Sunday excursions was harmless, wasn't it?

"Maybe you just want your half day to yourself," he said when she didn't immediately answer. "Totally understandable—"

"No, actually, it might be nice to have someone look at houses with me—it could save me from some of the Realtor's hard sell," Vonni heard herself say before she was completely sure she should. "And you can meet my dog." The dog that was going to come before any man!

Dane grinned as if she'd granted him his deepest wish. "Great! Why don't you let me pick you up so you won't have to drive—you can have the day off from that, too."

She cast a glance at the two-seater sports car she was

parked behind. "If that's yours it won't work—the sack of dog food I bring to the shelter every week is almost as big as that car. I have to have it carted out and lifted into my trunk at the store and someone burly has to bring it into the shelter."

"I'll bring my SUV instead."

"And you're sure you want to do this?" she asked, her confusion echoing in her tone.

"No doubt about it," he answered, his eyes meeting hers and staying there as if to let her know he meant it.

Or maybe there was more to it, because suddenly he didn't seem able to take his gaze off her and Vonni couldn't read his expression.

She only knew that she really liked looking at him. At his chiseled features and even that bump in the bridge of his nose. And that she never seemed to get enough of the sight of him....

Then he leaned forward and kissed her so lightly that his lips barely touched hers. So lightly and so quickly that it was over before it actually sank in that that was what he was doing. Before she could respond.

And he was back to looking into her eyes.

"You know," he said in a quiet, thoughtful way, "because I was the oldest of my part of the family, I felt like it was my particular job to keep Dylan and Derek and the triplets in line—my brothers and sisters. To make sure we weren't too much to handle. I guess maybe somewhere deep down I worried that GiGi might send us somewhere else if we were. So I toed the line and took 'being a good example' seriously. I tried not to misbehave myself. I reasoned and negotiated and made peace whenever there were fights—that's probably how I grew up to do the job I do," he added with a small chuckle. "I haven't done the conventional thing with my life, but still I don't rock the boat. I'm not a troublemaker—"

Why was he telling her all this at this moment?

"So how come," he went on, "here I am now, doing something I know better than to do with you?"

Aah... The kiss.

However small it had been, he knew he shouldn't have done it.

She knew he shouldn't have done it. Clients shouldn't be kissing her and she shouldn't be kissing clients. Even if the client wasn't the groom.

But she didn't hate that he had so she merely said, "I don't know, how come?" And then she wondered why the words had sounded flirty when that wasn't how she'd intended them.

"I don't know, either...." he said, his own voice quiet and deep—as if he might be about to kiss her again.

Maybe longer this time....

But he didn't. He caught himself at the last minute and stepped back instead.

Crushing her secret hopes.

She didn't let him know that, though. Or let herself think too much about it. Instead, she pushed off the hood of her car, went around to the driver's side and opened her door.

"Text me your address and tell me a time for tomorrow."

"Ten o'clock tomorrow morning?" Vonni answered.

"I'll be there."

"See you then," she said as she got behind the wheel and closed the door.

But as she drove around the fountain and headed away from the house she couldn't help wondering what it had all meant.

The kiss.

What he'd said after it.

The possibility that he might have been inclined to kiss her again....

And she couldn't help thinking just the tiniest, tiniest bit about Chrystal's suggestion.

That she have a fling with Dane Camden....

Chapter Six

"Hi, Mom."

Ever since Elizabeth Hunter had moved to Arizona and become busy with the new man in her life, it wasn't easy for her and Vonni to talk as much as they had in the past. So now they had a date every Sunday morning to catch up by video chat on their computers.

"Hi, honey." Elizabeth returned the greeting, settling in in front of the screen with her ever-present cup of coffee. "How was your week?"

"Busy. But interesting…." she said, realizing that she hadn't yet told Elizabeth anything about Dane. They'd just met on Monday, *after* the previous Sunday's call. Which struck her as strange because the way she was feeling about him made it seem as if she'd known him much, much longer than that.

It was probably just because they hadn't gone a day without seeing each other, she reasoned.

Vonni told her mother about meeting Dane, being hired to do Georgianna Camden's wedding and the other job offer.

"That sounds like a big opportunity," Elizabeth said, but with reservation in her voice. "After setting up wedding departments in all of their stores, you'd oversee them? Worldwide?"

"Apparently so."

"And leave Burke's...."

"I told Dane I'm perfectly happy there and should be made partner any day."

Vonni could see the concern on her mother's face as she sat there in pensive silence. Was it the idea of Vonni going to work for the family that had aided and abetted the crime against Elizabeth's father, or Vonni's long-held belief that she would be made partner in Burke's Weddings?

"Which part are you worried about?" she asked.

"Well, both. You know I always tell you not to count too much on that partnership. I just don't think it's going to happen."

"Mom—"

"I know, you think your friendship with Chrystal makes things different than they were for me, but I'm just not sure about that. To the Burkes we're employees—maybe that isn't how Chrystal sees you, but Mr. Burke is really who's in control and to him... Honey, we're nothing."

"You came away okay. You had enough to retire young when Mrs. Burke died."

"You know that's only because Mrs. Burke gave me bonuses and told me to invest them in whatever her husband was investing in, and to sell whenever he sold. I don't think he even knew what she was doing or that

I was following his footsteps. But it made me some money. When Mrs. Burke died Mr. Burke gave me two weeks' severance and showed me the door. His wife was gone, my services as her assistant were no longer needed and that was it for me. He didn't even say I could stay in the cottage until I found another place to live."

Vonni knew all of that. Her mother had stayed with her immediately after Mrs. Burke's funeral, and although she hadn't minded that, she hadn't appreciated or approved of how Chrystal's father had treated her mother. And even though her mother had pretended to excuse his actions by saying that he was grieving and probably hadn't wanted her around to remind him of his late wife, neither of them had believed it.

"Still, without me there isn't a Burke's Weddings," Vonni contended, despite what she'd said to Dane.

"It wouldn't be the same without you, but it would still exist," her mother said kindly. "Mr. Burke would just hire someone else to fill your shoes."

"So you think I should take the job with Camdens?"

Her mother's eyebrows arched and her expression was pained. "I don't know about that...."

"I've been told I can write my own ticket, include any provisions in my contract that make me comfortable and secure."

"I suppose that's something," Elizabeth said, obviously unconvinced. "But trusting them? I've heard that the new guard is all about doing good, but how far from the tree can the apple really fall?"

"I'm working with Dane Camden—he's Mrs. Camden's go-between for planning her wedding, and he also made the job offer and is trying to sell me on it. He seems pretty straightforward. I haven't seen any indications that he *isn't* on the up-and-up."

"And Grampa thought that turning down H. J. Camden's offer for his formulas was enough to keep them out of Camden hands."

"It would have been if Phil hadn't stolen them and sold them."

"Or did the Camdens just enlist Phil to do the dirty work?"

It was a debate her family had been having for as long as Vonni could remember.

"The rich are different than you and me, Vonni, and I have to wonder if the Camdens are going to lure you in, take all your ideas and expertise for themselves and then let you just be roadkill the way they did Grampa."

"I don't know," Vonni admitted. "Dane claims their executive agreements include a golden-parachute clause that's unrivaled."

"But you have to consider the source of that information."

"All I do know," Vonni said, "is that the two Camdens who bought Grampa's stolen formulas aren't around anymore and I haven't heard anything alarming in the job offer from the one who is."

"So you're leaning toward taking it?" her mother asked in surprise.

Vonni was afraid she was leaning toward Dane himself.

"No, I've barely even thought about it because I've just had too much going on this week," she said honestly.

"And you've had your heart set on becoming a partner in Burke's Weddings all these years," her mother added knowingly, but with some trepidation still in her tone.

"I'm also a little worried about what will happen to Burke's Weddings even if I don't take the job with

Camdens—if Camden Superstores start offering the same services they could run us out of business."

"The way they have businesses before you," Elizabeth confirmed. "That's something to think about. I'd say that if the shop really was Chrystal's baby, Mr. Burke would keep it going no matter what to make her happy. But since she couldn't care less about it and it's really your shop, if profits drop because of Camdens, he'll shut you down—don't doubt it for a minute, honey."

This was not turning into an uplifting conversation so Vonni decided to change the subject. "How was your week?"

Her mother's expression brightened remarkably. "Oh, Audie and I had a fabulous week! We found a new condo and we'll be moving the first of the month."

Elizabeth and her new man-friend—as she called him—had decided to move in together.

Vonni's mother leaned close to the computer camera and whispered, "I think a proposal is on the way—I caught him looking in the jewelry-store window at the mall yesterday. His son Dashell came in for a visit and I think Audie wanted to tell him before he pops the question."

"And what would your answer be?" Vonni asked without any real doubt as to the answer.

"I'd say yes!" Elizabeth gushed, sitting back so Vonni could see more than her nose and mouth on the screen. "Of course, I'll make sure there's a prenuptial agreement to protect what money I have—that goes to you and no one else when I die."

"I just want you to be happy," Vonni said, glad that after the kind of marriage her parents had had, and after being left to raise her alone, her mother might have finally found the reward for her lifetime of toil and trouble.

"I wanted to talk to you about Dashell," Elizabeth said then, with intrigue in her voice. "He's single. A lawyer. And he lives in Denver…."

"Not in the market right now, Mom," Vonni reminded.

"I know, but you have to strike while the iron is hot, honey. He's never been married and he's about to turn forty. Audie really wants him to settle down and he's sure if Dashell just met the right girl—"

"In other words, Dashell isn't interested *himself* in settling down, his father just thinks he should. And that makes him like way, way too many of the other guys I've dated and tried to be the *right girl* for—he's what I'm on hiatus *from,* Mom. And exactly what I want to avoid wasting any more time with when I do go back to the manhunt."

"But you're perfect for—"

"It doesn't matter. I've been perfect for a lot of them. A lot of them have been perfect for me. Or so I've thought. But when marriage and family aren't what they want or what they're ready for, there's no changing that. And waiting and putting off what *I* want, and trying to show them the appeal of a wife and family and hoping they'll come around just doesn't work. Or when they come around, they come around with someone else. One way or another, I've learned my lesson and I'm not doing it again. I swear I'm not. When I get back to dating it's only going to be with men who are genuinely looking for the same thing I am. And I'm not going back to it until I've had some Vonni time and gotten some of the things I've been putting off."

"You're just tired," her mother said, but it sounded

as if her only regret was her timing in presenting the latest Mr. Right. She didn't seem to be taking anything Vonni said seriously.

"I will *never* be ready for the kind of guy Dashell sounds like. Never again," Vonni proclaimed forcefully.

But she was picturing Dane when she said it and feeling a little sorry that he also fit the bill of the go-nowhere guy. For all she knew, Dane's grandmother was out in the world saying that she just wanted *him* to settle down and knew that if *he* could only meet the right girl he would want to.

And too many girls who heard it would be hoping *they* were the right girl and give it a try.

But Vonni wasn't one of them. Not anymore. Not when it came to Dane. Not when it came to this Dashell. Not when it came to anyone.

It was just so much easier to nip it in the bud when her mother was trying to fix her up with someone she'd never met than when she was spending a whole lot of time with someone she found fun and thoughtful and interesting and good-natured and charismatic and per-sonable and oh, so sexy....

Someone who was exactly the kind of guy she envi-sioned building a life with.

Someone she'd already found herself wanting to kiss, then actually kissing, and then wanting to kiss again.

Maybe she should start therapy during her husband-hunt hiatus and see if outside help could figure out why she always attracted—and was attracted to—these go-nowhere guys....

"So are you really not seeing *anyone?*" her mother asked.

"I'm seeing Charlie this afternoon."

"The girl dog with the boy's name that you're keeping at the pound until you get a house," her mother said, proving she did hear some of what Vonni told her.

"Right."

"But you haven't found a house yet?"

"I have three to look at today."

"With the Realtor you're not interested in, either...."

"With the Realtor I'm not interested in, either," Vonni confirmed. She'd previously dashed her mother's hopes that the single male Realtor might change Vonni's mind about avoiding men and dating.

Vonni heard her mother's name being called in the background and then she saw Elizabeth's white-haired companion come into the room. She watched her mother's youthfully attractive face light up at the sight of him and was glad that Elizabeth had met someone she was compatible and happy with. For her mother's sake and because it gave her hope for herself.

"Say hi to Vonni, Audie," her mother instructed.

"Hi, Vonni!" he said more loudly than he needed to, waving madly at the computer so that for a moment there was nothing to be seen but a big blurry palm going back and forth.

"Hi, Audie," Vonni answered, exchanging pleasantries with him.

She knew that once he was with her mother that her mother would want to focus on him, so it came as no surprise when Elizabeth said that she'd let Vonni get going on her day and they ended the call.

Not that Vonni minded.

She *did* want to get going on her day.

Because in spite of knowing better, she couldn't wait to get the day that she was spending with Dane underway....

* * *

"So this is Casual Vonni—sandals, jeans, a couple of T-shirts and the hair down.... Very nice. I like it."

Vonni was never comfortable with compliments. She was happy to get them but they just embarrassed her. And Dane's quick look, traveling from her red-polished toes to her free-falling hair, only made her more self-conscious.

"It's my day off...sort of," she responded, knowing full well that if she weren't meeting Dane, she wouldn't have worn the best jeans she owned, the lacy camisole under her most expensive teal-green scoop-neck T-shirt or her strappy flat sandals. It was more like casual-date wear than going-to-the-animal-shelter-to-spend-time-with-her-dog wear.

But she *was* also working, so she couldn't go *too* casual. Or so she'd reasoned when she bypassed what she would ordinarily have worn in favor of this outfit.

"I'm glad to see that you didn't dress up, either—the animal shelter is a little like going to the zoo," she added then, giving him her own once-over.

He also had on jeans—faded and aged and broken in but not sloppy at all—and a plain white mock-neck T-shirt with long sleeves that he'd pushed to his elbows.

He was clean-shaven and smelled of a citrusy cologne. And even wearing nothing fancy, he still managed to look terrific with his broad shoulders and muscular chest filling out the shirt just right, and jeans that hugged his hips and thick thighs to perfection.

"Jeans on Sunday are a treat—GiGi won't allow them at her dinners, so even though I get out of a suit, jeans are still off-limits."

"And you went to the trouble of parking—I was trying to save you from that," she added.

The three-story six-plex she rented an apartment in was just blocks outside of Denver on a street crammed with other apartment buildings. There was only street parking available for visitors and she hadn't wanted to inconvenience him with having to search for a spot, so she'd told him she would meet him in front. But when she'd reached the foot of the outdoor stairs that shared an alcove with the other second-floor apartment he was already only a few steps away.

"No big deal," he said as if it really wasn't.

Had this been part of her husband hunt, he would have become a likelier candidate due to his courtesy and taking the parking situation in stride. She appreciated a man who would go out of his way a little for her, and someone who didn't make mountains out of molehills also seemed like good husband and father material.

But she reminded herself that her husband hunt was suspended, and that he was self-proclaimed nonhusband, nonfather material, and told herself not to forget it!

He pointed out his SUV across the street and down the block, and they headed in that direction.

"I thought we could shop for the baskets first," she told him along the way. "Then if you change your mind and want to opt out of the rest of what I need to do today you can just bring me back for my car and have the afternoon free."

"I won't change my mind," he said as if there was no question about it, unlocking and opening his passenger door for her when they reached the vehicle.

And as much as Vonni knew it was a bad sign, it pleased her no end to think he really was serious about spending the entire day with her.

He advised her to buckle up and closed her door, then rounded the rear of the SUV and got behind the wheel.

"Where to?" he asked as he put the key in the ignition and turned on the engine.

"One of your stores," she told him, having decided in advance that that was probably the route she should go despite the fact that she frequented smaller boutiques for other clients. "Camden Superstores sells baskets and everything else we can put in them to welcome and make your out-of-town guests feel more at home. So I guess whichever one you want to go to."

"Colorado Boulevard it is," he proclaimed, heading back toward downtown. "It'll also give you a chance to take a look around and see all the other things you'd have at your disposal in the stores if you came to work planning weddings for us."

Vonni didn't comment and instead said, "So…is there a special red carpet rolled out when a Camden walks into one of these places?"

He laughed. "Hmm…maybe we should start doing that."

"Lights don't flash, bells and whistles don't go off when you walk through the door? There's no security escort?" Vonni taunted him a little more.

He laughed again. "I know, it's disappointing," he said in mock outrage. "I'm going to have to see what I can do about getting more perks."

There were a few perks, though.

In this area of the city, a smallish, defunct shopping mall had been taken over, remodeled and turned into one giant Camdens. Rather than parking in the enormous—and crowded—lot in front, he pulled around to the rear and parked nose first to the building right beside a metal door that he had a key to.

Once inside they went to an office area where he greeted security and the day's manager by their first names, introduced her and said they'd be doing some shopping.

And after gathering baskets, everything Vonni recommended to fill them, plus cellophane to wrap them in and ribbon to tie the cellophane at the top, the manager took their purchases to check out himself.

While he did that, Dane told Vonni where he thought the wedding departments should be located in the stores, and how they could be enclosed to isolate them and decorated in the same elegant fashion as her shop.

"That way your brides will step into a whole different world like they do in your shop. We can have the wedding gowns presented to them there, you can do your food tasting the way we did the other night. They can sit and look at examples or pictures of flower arrangements, decorations, what have you. And even though everything will be coming from Camdens, they won't be out in the departments shopping off racks or shelves. They'll still have their special handling and treatment, and feel as if they're getting their moment in the spotlight."

Vonni merely nodded. On one hand, she was happy that was what he envisioned if she did go to work for him. But she knew that if brides could find that kind of environment and treatment through Camdens, it could severely cut into the business of shops like Burke's Weddings.

She discovered the final perk of being with a Camden at a Camden Superstore was that their purchases were all loaded into the back of Dane's SUV for them. So the entire process wasn't quite like Vonni's usual shopping experience.

From there they went to meet Vonni's Realtor at the first house she was slated to look at and then moved on to the next two.

The first was a nice Georgian two-story but it was more house than Vonni was looking for. The second was a tri-level that seemed chopped up and had far more stairs than she was willing to deal with, and the third was a small ranch-style that needed a little work.

As she'd hoped, Dane was helpful in deflecting some of the Realtor's hard sell. But he was also insightful and observant, pointing out positives and negatives in each place and making it the best time Vonni had had yet looking at potential new homes.

Despite the work it needed, the third house had the feel of home to her. She could see herself there in a way she hadn't been able to in anything else. She loved the French doors that led to the back yard that was perfect for her dog, plus the living room was warm and cozy— she envisioned snuggling up on her couch in front of a fire in the fireplace with a good book on a snowy Sunday afternoon.

That all told her it was the right house for her, and when she decided to make an offer, it was especially nice of Dane to say he'd help her do some of the minor repairs that it needed—which, in her excitement, she told him she'd take him up on.

They had a fast-food lunch in the car on the way to the pet-supply store. By then things between them had become so relaxed that—at Dane's request—Vonni fed him French fries as he drove. They bantered back and forth, teasing each other as they went.

At the pet-supply store Dane was able to lift the largest bag of dog food without help. And while Vonni had never been impressed by the teenage boys who usually did it, today she couldn't help devouring the sight of Dane's muscles flexing.

She was subtle in her ogling, but subtle or not, it was impossible not to admire the display of power and strength, even though he didn't seem to be aware of it himself.

Then they headed for the animal shelter.

It was a privately owned shelter with a no-kill policy—that was why Vonni supported it, and she explained that to Dane along the way.

"So what happens to the animals who aren't adopted?" he asked.

"They just live at the shelter. The staff and foster families will take them home for overnights and weekends sometimes, then bring them back, but one way or another they aren't put down."

What that also meant was that the shelter ended up with a lot of long-term pets with disabilities because the animals with disabilities were the least likely to find homes.

"That's why I'm taking Charlie. A fight with a cat cost her one of her eyes," Vonni told him on the way in.

"Your dog only has one eye?"

"It's not a big deal. She still has the other one."

Dane laughed yet again but cast her a glance that seemed to say he was doing a little admiring of his own.

Charlie was a three-year-old female schnauzer. Despite the fact that she had to stay at the shelter for now, she knew that she belonged to Vonni because the minute Vonni went in the front doors of the shelter's reception area Charlie started to yip and howl from the back.

"Charlie always tells us when you're here," the shelter worker said as he came through the door behind the counter.

"Hi, Mac." Vonni introduced the shelter worker to Dane.

The two men exchanged greetings and then Mac held up the mutt he was carrying. "And this is Ralph. Someone found him trying to get into their trash for food. He's a scrappy little guy. Maybe part terrier with this squarish face and brown-and-black coloring, and part Welsh corgi or dachshund because of the long body and short legs."

Ralph took the introduction seriously and lunged out of Mac's arms toward Dane.

Acting fast, Dane caught him.

"He isn't your dog, is he?" Mac asked, watching as Ralph settled into Dane's arms as if he belonged there.

"Maybe he just wants to be," Vonni said.

But Dane's only response was to pet the dog behind the ear and say, "Hi, fella."

Which Vonni thought was probably par for the course—the man was anticommitment after all.

He continued to give Ralph attention, though. He brought the mutt along when Vonni led him to the rear of the shelter to get Charlie and together they took the two dogs into the small grassy courtyard where Vonni played with Charlie every week.

Dane got down on the lawn with her and the two dogs, and between their lighthearted chatter and playing with the animals, they managed to stay until Mac reappeared to tell them the shelter was closing for the night.

Vonni gave Charlie a lengthy goodbye and told her she thought she might have found them a place to live so she could come home with her. Then both dogs went with Mac, Vonni took a deep, steeling breath to get her out of there without the dog she'd come to love and she and Dane left.

"It breaks my heart to see you leave your dog behind," Dane confided as they got back into his SUV and headed for her shop to drop off the day's purchases.

"It breaks my heart, too."

"Could we sneak her into your condo? If somebody turns you in to your landlord you could say you're just dog-sitting."

Vonni laughed. "I already tried both of those things," she said, appreciating his concern nevertheless. "There's a two-day limit for keeping someone else's pet and my neighbor across the landing—Mrs. Dunwilly—keeps track. She's who turned me in the last time I tried to take Charlie home. Besides, Charlie is a barker—that's the other thing that upset Mrs. Dunwilly."

"How about my house? I don't have much of a yard—just a patch of grass—but it would be enough for a temporary thing. You want to keep her there?"

"Mrs. Dunwilly? Absolutely!" Vonni had intentionally misunderstood, making him laugh again.

"I like you a lot, but I don't know if I like you enough to take in your cranky neighbor," he said with an affectionate glance. "Your dog—yes. But Mrs. Dunwilly? Not a chance."

"Scared of a little seventy-nine-year-old busybody?"

"Terrified."

"You probably should be. She's looking for Husband Number Five and I'd bet she'd trample right over your no-marriage-ever rule. Or seduce you out of it...."

"Eww...." He laughed and groaned and grimaced and made Vonni laugh once more, too. "Seventy-*nine?*" he repeated. "She's older than my *grandmother!*"

"Only a few years, and your grandmother is getting married," Vonni reminded him.

"You know, sometimes I think there's a little bit of a mean streak in you," he countered as he pulled into the small lot behind her shop. "But I still stand by my offer—Charlie can stay at my house until you get into your own."

It was a nice suggestion, but not one that Vonni could accept. Something had happened today to make things between them seem even more friendly and familiar than they'd already become. Hardly any formality from the business association was left and, in fact, if she thought too much about it, she knew that today could easily have qualified as a really good extended date. But that was all dangerous and letting him keep her dog made it even worse.

So as they began to unload his SUV she said, "Thanks, but Charlie is familiar with the shelter and it's probably better not to disrupt her with two moves."

"Well, if you change your mind…"

She wouldn't. Any more than he was likely to change his mind about his no-marriage-ever vow.

Which was a shame. Because what the day with him had shown her once again was how much there was about the man to recommend him….

After dropping off the baskets and their contents, Dane insisted on buying Vonni dinner. He suggested La Loma—a Mexican restaurant blocks from her apartment. But the fact that he could park near her apartment and they could walk was not the only reason Vonni let him talk her into it.

Not even hours and hours with him had made her ready to end the day, and by then she'd given up trying to deny how much she was enjoying being with him.

They'd both been to La Loma before and agreed that it had the best green chili in town. They also agreed that the margaritas were wonderful, and they liked so many of the same foods on the menu that they decided to order the green enchiladas and the chili rellenos and split them.

Over dinner Dane reassured her that she'd done the right thing in making an offer on the house they'd looked at, and let her know he loved her dog but resisted when she urged him to adopt Ralph. On the whole they talked and talked and laughed and laughed until well into the night before either of them noticed they were the last customers there.

Even then Dane didn't seem any more eager than Vonni to call it a night, but it was obvious that they had to so he paid the check and they headed for her apartment.

"I don't know when I've had a day I liked as much as this one," Dane said on the way.

She wished that wasn't true for her, too, but it was. They hadn't done anything she wouldn't have ordinarily done by herself, but she was well aware of how much more fun it had been with his company.

His company—because she'd spent days like this one with other men she was in relationships with, relationships she'd been convinced were going somewhere serious, and never had she enjoyed any one of those days as much as she'd enjoyed this one with Dane. Being with him just wasn't like what she'd found with anyone else....

"Thanks for letting me tag along," he was saying, breaking into her thoughts.

"Thanks for tagging along—it was fun," she countered as if it had been insignificant when it sooo hadn't been. At least not to her.

"And what excuse should I use to see you tomorrow?" he asked, sounding hopeful.

Vonni laughed lightly at his wording. "Club hopping," she said.

"On a Monday night?"

"We're on a time crunch, remember? Actually, it's more like *lounge* hopping—you said your grandmother and her fiancé want romantic music from the fifties and sixties. I contacted the people I use to hire bands and orchestras and they have a quartet playing tomorrow night at a *lounge* in Larimer Square—"

"So no *hopping,* just one *lounge?*"

"Unless you don't like them and then my booker told me about a trio playing in a hotel bar on Colfax, and a Frank Sinatra sound-alike working in lower downtown."

"We'll hope the first group is *great!*" Dane said with exaggerated enthusiasm.

"Not a big fan of romantic music of the fifties and sixties?" she asked with yet another laugh.

"I can honestly say that I don't own any."

"Maybe this will broaden your horizons."

"Anything is possible," he said dubiously, laughing once more and making Vonni realize that they'd done a whole lot of that today.

They were coming up to his SUV parked on the street and she told him she could go the rest of the way to her apartment on her own. But he wouldn't hear of it and walked her to her six-plex, up the wooden stairs and to her door.

Where she was extremely tempted to ask him in.

But the day had almost been *too* good, and she was a little worried what might happen if she did.

So rather than doing that she showed him her keys and said, "Okay, safe and sound at my door." Then she nodded in the direction of the apartment that faced hers and whispered, "Probably with Mrs. Dunwilly watching through her peephole."

"Aah...Mrs. Dunwilly..." he said as if he was intrigued.

"Should I introduce you?"

"You'd do it, too, wouldn't you—if I said yes? Like feeding me French fries when I didn't think you would, and rolling around in the grass with dogs like a kid, and the poems or whatever those things were—"

"Ditties," she corrected, using her grandfather's terminology for what were the slightly off-color limericks he'd taught her. "I don't even know how you got me to recite those for you." But he had, in the car between looking at houses.

"I knew 'Lidia The Tattooed Lady,' but the rest?"

"My grandfather learned them in the army and he used to say them all the time. They just stuck."

Dane grinned and shook his head. "You just aren't like the women I usually hang out with."

"The Chrystal Burkes? I like Chrystal but no, I've never been much like her or her other friends."

"You're kind of a breath of fresh air."

"Don't ever tell one of your girlfriends that they're stale air or you'll completely blow your image as a good guy," she advised.

"You don't think I'm really a good guy?" he challenged.

That was part of the trouble—she *did* think he was a good guy. A really good guy.

Who didn't want what she wanted in life....

So why didn't she just say good-night and leave him on her doorstep? Why was she prolonging this time with him by staying there, looking up into those blue eyes of his and wanting so badly for him to want what she wanted?

Wanting so badly to have him kiss her again....

"I do think you're a good guy." She admitted that much. But very quietly. Then, because she didn't want to get herself in too deeply, she added more playfully, "You must be, you're like the Pied Piper when it comes to kids and dogs—Charlie and Ralph and that other big dog that came in as we were leaving the shelter all loved you, and everywhere we went today kids singled you out as if you were Santa Claus—"

"It's probably the beard," he said, rubbing his chin where it was stubbled with five-o'clock shadow that only made him all the more ruggedly sexy.

And oh, but she wanted things with him to be different!

So much it was almost an ache inside of her....

Then she did get one of the things she wanted—he raised a big hand to cup her jawline, tipped her face up and kissed her.

It almost made it worse for her, though, because unlike the quickie of the night before, this one was a great kiss. A tremendous kiss. A perfect kiss.

Firm but not too firm. Lips parted but not too far. The tiniest bit moist—just enough. And a hint of a sway to it that made her drift away, lost in it....

Until it was over and Vonni almost forgot to open her eyes, remembering to at the last second and finding him studying her when she did.

His hand was still on her face, his thumb brushing her cheek ever so lightly. And his expression was thoughtful and maybe a little stunned, too, as if he'd found something there, between them, that he hadn't anticipated.

Before he could regroup.

He took his hand away. He stood straighter and away from her. And he gave her a small, more reserved smile. "Thanks for today," he said.

Vonni wasn't sure she could trust her voice, so she merely returned his smile.

Then he turned and went down the stairs and Vonni forced herself to unlock her door and go into her apartment.

But somehow even once she was inside with her door closed behind her, she felt as if she'd still brought a little part of him with her.

The faint scent of his cologne.

The warmth of his hand on her face.

The feel of his lips on hers....

And tonight there weren't as many shouldn't-haves torturing her as there were couldn't-haves.

Because hate it though she might, she knew without a doubt that Dane was someone with whom she couldn't have what she truly wanted.

Even when, more and more, she did seem to want him in spite of herself....

Chapter Seven

On Monday night after Vonni and Dane had both worked late, Vonni found a way to kill two birds with one stone. The bartender she was recommending to Dane was working at a restaurant across from the Larimer Square lounge where the quartet they were checking out was playing.

This time Vonni insisted that she buy Dane dinner, which they ate at the bar while the bartender made samples of his specialty drinks for them to taste.

A sip here, a sip there, no more than a sip, but by the time the meal was finished Vonni was very relaxed. So relaxed that when they stepped out of the restaurant as darkness was just falling, she lost sight of the fact that she wasn't on a date and grabbed Dane's arm to stop him so they could watch the canopy of white streetlights coming on overhead.

The lights set the historic street apart from other

Denver streets, but all she could really think about in the moment was her hold on Dane. She was grasping his bare forearm—thick and warm and strong—and she knew she had no business making this kind of contact, let alone liking the feel of it as much as she did.

She forced herself to let go and watched as the rest of the lights went on. Then she commanded herself to get back to business and only business.

But as they started to cross the street, Dane placed a hand to her back. And while more alarms went off in her head, she still couldn't help enjoying that sensation of physical contact.

Or moving a little closer to his side.

The Larimer Lounge was down a flight of stairs bordered by a wrought iron railing. Dane kept his hand on her back as they went from the sidewalk into the stairwell. At the foot of the stairs he opened the single door to the place and urged her in ahead of him.

That was when he broke contact, and Vonni fought a pang of disappointment even as she told herself to quit it.

Inside they were faced with a small bar in a square pit. A hostess greeted them and took them around the bar to one of the tables that surrounded the dance floor.

The basement establishment was dimly lit, with scant light over the bar, over the dance floor and only slightly brighter light over the bandstand where the Fisher Quartet had already begun to play.

The place wasn't overly crowded and the clientele tended to be older. But Dane didn't seem to mind as he held out her chair for her and then took the one next to it for himself so that they were both facing the stage.

"The singer has a good voice," he observed after the waitress had brought them their order of two iced teas and they'd listened to a song. "He has that old crooner sound. GiGi likes that. I'm going to have her listen…."

He placed the call and after getting his grandmother on the line, held his cell phone in the direction of the singer for a few minutes.

Then, he said into the phone, "What do you think?" And after a pause, "Okay, sure, put him on." He held the phone out a second time, presumably for the groom to listen, as well.

That went on for a few minutes before they had the go-ahead for the band.

"So we don't need the other two stops tonight?" Vonni asked, fighting another wave of disappointment at the thought that the evening could end soon.

"Nope, we're home free. But we'd better drink the tea and dilute all those booze samples," he answered.

That bought her at least a little while longer and Vonni told herself she was only glad because she liked the music her grandfather had taught her to dance to.

Dane leaned toward her then and said, "You know—"

But that was as far as he got before a tiny, very old white-haired man in a dapper suit came up from behind them and said to him, "Around here if you waste a girl like that by not dancing with her, somebody'll steal her from you. Maybe me…." The man winked at Vonni and made her laugh.

"Thanks for the warning," Dane said, playing along before looking to Vonni again. "That was what I was just about to ask you, anyway. Dance with me?"

She was tempted to deny his request, but she was slightly worried that the elegantly dressed elderly gentleman really would ask her to dance. And she could tell just sitting there that she would be inches taller than he was, even in the ballet-style shoes she was wearing, which matched her black slacks and white blouse perfectly.

So she nodded at Dane, who took her hand in his, led her onto the floor and swung her into his arms.

And she had to admit, it was great to resume the physical contact that had started when she'd reached for his arm on the street.

He pulled her just close enough so their bodies were touching ever so lightly, and she silently shouted at herself, *He's a client!* Plus, she should be sticking to her goal of steering clear of men for a while.

But it didn't matter. She continued to feel excited and happy and content and complete, as if there wasn't a single thing about this that was wrong.

Dangerous feelings that she tried not to dwell on as she said, "Thanks for saving me."

"The old guy just gave me the excuse," Dane answered, smiling down at her.

He was clean-shaven and smelled of that cologne she liked. He was also a very good dancer and Vonni was itching to rest her cheek on his chest. But she managed to combat that inclination by reminding herself that while she might not have a handle on what was going on with her when it came to this guy, she was still out with a client. If she was going to write off the dinner she'd paid for, she certainly couldn't be snuggling up to him on the dance floor.

No matter how much she wanted to.

With occasional pauses to drink their iced teas, Dane kept her dancing for more than an hour before he saw something over her head and bent close to her ear to say, "I think if we don't get out of here I'm about to be cut in on."

And while Vonni wasn't thrilled to have to stop, if

she wasn't dancing with Dane, she didn't want to dance at all. So she agreed and before her elderly suitor could get to her, they were back out on the street.

"Okay," Vonni said as they headed for the lot where Dane's sports car was parked. "Now we have music and a bartender for the wedding. You've picked everything out, invitations are sent, flowers are ordered, we have a venue, a caterer, a menu, a cake and nameplates and gift baskets that I'll do this week. We've actually managed to get through my to-do list, and that means your part is done. Now it's up to me and the suppliers and vendors who have promised to put a super-rush on everything."

She'd realized earlier in the day that tonight might be the end of getting to spend any concentrated amount of time with him. But coming to this moment still hit her harder than it should have, and she felt such a wave of despondency wash through her that it nearly leveled her. But she couldn't let him know that.

The fact that he'd finished his part in planning his grandmother's wedding seemed to come as a surprise to Dane. His eyebrows were arched as he opened the passenger door for her and then closed it again after she'd gotten in.

He went around to the driver's side and slipped behind the wheel before he said, "I have two things I still need to talk to you about.... But really? Tonight is it? I thought you and I would be racing all the way to the finish line."

"I'll be doing that, but it isn't true for you. After you've chosen everything—and now you have—I take it from here. So you're off the hook."

He started the engine and then said with some disbelief, "I won't see you until things get going at the end of the week?"

"When I do the setup and staging at your grandmother's house, yes," she confirmed. "I'll do most of that on Friday and a few things on Saturday before the wedding."

"Well, I didn't know that," he complained. "I mean, I knew about the setup—we discussed that. But there's really no more for me to do between now and then?"

Vonni laughed slightly. "I thought you'd be thrilled…."

He frowned.

"What two things did you need to talk to me about?" she asked, remembering what he'd said.

He didn't answer for a moment as he pulled out of the parking lot, then he said, "I think I needed some warning for this. I'm not ready to be done…."

With the wedding planning or with her?

It seemed odd that he should lament being finished with his part in the wedding planning.

But Vonni couldn't believe—or let herself believe—that he wasn't ready to be done with her.

"How about if we take a drive?" he suggested then. "It's beautiful out, we can cruise a little, maybe park somewhere and put the top down…."

Vonni had already worked a fifteen-hour day. She had to be at the shop by seven o'clock the next morning and would be in the last crunch for the rest of the week for a Thursday-evening wedding, a Saturday-afternoon wedding and his grandmother's wedding on Saturday evening. Surely he could tell her the two things he needed to tell her on the way to her shop where her own car was parked, so there was absolutely no reason she should say yes.

But she did.

"And then you'll tell me those other two things?"

"I will," he said, holding out.

He left Larimer Square and the city behind and was on the highway within minutes, headed west.

That was when he said, "GiGi called tonight just before we left and wanted me to ask if you could have the caterers do a brunch for us on Sunday at the house. I know, this is really last-minute. But it doesn't need to be anything big or flashy. She just thought it would be nice for our out-of-towners to have a send-off. She also thought that if the same caterers who do the wedding, do the brunch, the overlap might help.... What do you think? Any chance?"

"I can talk to the caterers." Vonni knew they would bend over backward to do it. They were thrilled to have the Camdens' business and hoped to be hired by them again in the future so they were likely to be accommodating. "If they do omelet and crepe stations so the food is cooked on-site, that cuts down on advance preparations," she added. "And the trays and serving things will already be there—along with some other equipment they could probably use, and supplies and ingredients that they'd need both times.... It might be workable if they aren't already booked for something else and can get enough staff...."

"That would be great. We're fine with anything. I know this is even more incredibly short notice than the wedding was, so whatever it takes, whatever it costs."

"I'll talk to them first thing in the morning and let you know."

He got off the highway and drove through a quiet suburban neighborhood with large old houses set far back from the streets behind well-manicured lawns. Winding through the scenic area where huge trees reached their full branches overhead, they passed a pristine golf course with a stately clubhouse that could be seen in the distance. Then he turned onto a street Vonni hadn't even noticed was there and went up a steep hill that took them into a small park that looked out at some of the highest peaks of the Rocky Mountains.

They were the only car in the lot when he pulled into a prime spot, pushed a button that caused the car's soft-top to rise and then fold away behind them before he turned off the engine.

"This is nice. I've never been here," Vonni said, looking out at the suburban lights below them with the silhouette of the mountains and the clear, star-strewn sky as a backdrop.

"I came up here a lot in high school...." he said with insinuation in his tone.

"To be alone with girls," Vonni goaded.

He angled to face her, stretched his arm across the top of her headrest and merely smiled, neither confirming or denying anything.

"The second thing I wanted to talk to you about is Friday night," he said instead.

"Don't tell me you want the caterers to do the rehearsal dinner now, too, because I don't think that's as workable as a last-minute brunch."

"No, the food's all taken care of."

"I told you I'll make sure we're finished with the setup and out by the time you have the rehearsal so we won't disturb anything," she said, trying to anticipate any problems.

"I remember—although I didn't realize I wouldn't be seeing you between now and then. I figured tonight you'd tell me what we needed to do for the wedding tomorrow night, and the night after that and the night after that, and we'd spend this week the way we spent last week…."

Together.

Deep down Vonni wished that was the case, but she squashed the feeling as soon as she recognized it.

"Anyway," he went on, "what I wanted to talk about is you coming to the rehearsal dinner Friday night. Margaret is cooking the whole thing herself as a gift to GiGi—it'll just be family, along with the judge who's going to do the ceremony and his wife, and—"

"Oh, no, thank you, but I don't do that," Vonni said before he could go on. "Even when I'm coordinating the ceremony, too, I do the rehearsal, then leave before the dinner so I can gear up for the big day."

"Still—"

"The rehearsal dinner is a private event," Vonni continued. "Close family, the wedding party…. I don't feel like the wedding planner belongs at that."

"You can belong because you'll be with me—come as my date."

Worse yet…

And not only because it crossed the line between herself and a client—the line she kept kicking herself for not adhering to more faithfully—but also because attending the rehearsal dinner would mean she was not only working for the family that had helped swindle her own, but was socializing with them, too.

"I'm sure you have a legion of women better suited to be your date to your grandmother's rehearsal dinner," she concluded.

"A legion?" he repeated.

"At least. You're a hot commodity."

He laughed. "I don't know if that's as good as it sounds—what am I, a piece of meat?"

If he was a piece of meat he was the choicest cut she'd ever seen. But she wasn't going to say that. Instead, she said, "I've been told that being with you feeds the soul, so maybe in that sense.... Rumor has it that you're a great spirit lifter. That you make the women you're with feel good about themselves."

Vonni certainly couldn't refute that because it was how she felt whenever she was with him. He made her feel as if he appreciated her intelligence, her abilities, her insight. As if he found her interesting, attractive, witty, intriguing and just about everything she hoped she was. Being with Dane made her feel special, as if he saw things in her that other people—other men— might miss. Things of value.

And they were just together for business. She could only imagine what women came away with when he was wooing them. The man just had some kind of skill that other men she'd known lacked.

But she didn't want to say that, either.

"Where are you getting this stuff?" he asked.

"My brides and their bridesmaids talk. And sometimes you're the subject," she informed him. "You seem to have dated a lot of them...."

He gave her a look that said he wasn't going to talk about that, so she opted to veer slightly off the conversational path they were on and use the talk of his serial dating to satisfy her curiosity about something else.

"Have you always been so—" she wasn't sure what word to use and settled on "—casual about women?"

"Casual?"

"You know—have you always avoided serious relationships because you don't want to get married?"

"Who says I've avoided relationships? What do you

think, that my life is just a series of one-night stands or a different woman for every day of the week?"

That was how gossip had made it sound.

"It isn't? You don't avoid relationships?" Vonni challenged.

"I avoid relationships—and even dating—anyone who's actively looking for a husband and the whole domestic package."

Her....

"But I've had—and will have again—relationships with women who aren't looking for that. Who can get involved, enjoy the ride while it lasts—for months or even years—before we go our separate ways. And in between finding those kinds of relationships, I date just like everyone else does, until I find someone else I want to focus on for a while."

"And then you're monogamous?"

"I never juggle women."

"I guess I haven't heard it all," she admitted.

"And you just figured—what? That I run through women like water and sleep with every one of them?"

"I never hear anything bad about you like that. But yes, I did sort of assume that, well, you're a guy—you sleep around. One woman one night, a different one the next...."

He smiled as if he was enjoying dashing her assumptions about him. "So you think I've slept with every woman I've dated?"

"Maybe most of them?" she said, finding it difficult to believe that every woman he'd been with hadn't slept with him—especially as she sat close beside him, looking at how moonlight dusted the sharply defined features that made him one of the most handsome men she'd ever known. She was looking into eyes so blue it was as if they'd drained the sky of color. And broad, broad shoulders and a chest she still wanted to press her cheek to even though they weren't dancing anymore. Of course she'd assumed that he'd slept with every woman he'd ever dated—he was hard to resist.

"But you haven't?" she asked.

"I'm actually very selective about who I get that far with. My grandmother raised me to treat women right, not to be some kind of hound."

So maybe that was why his reputation—although colorful—wasn't a bad one. Why no one seemed to come away with a grudge against him. Why he was known as an ego booster, but not as a womanizer or a philanderer or a cad or a creep.

"You're not indiscriminate," Vonni said.

"No, I'm not. If that's what you've heard, somebody's lying."

"I haven't heard that," she assured him. "I just figured that as much as you get around—"

"I must really be getting around…."

"Right," Vonni admitted a bit contritely.

"Nope. I make sure that whoever I'm with knows where I stand and if it gets as far as the bedroom, that still isn't a—"

"Commitment to something more," Vonni filled in for him, knowing that she was guilty herself of making assumptions that men were more committed than they were, and reading too much into what went on with them. It was one of her regrets and part of what she'd sworn to stop doing when she returned to her search for a mate.

"So would you say you're particularly careful about who you take as far as the bedroom—that that's what makes it a relationship for you?" she asked, her curiosity about him growing rather than being satisfied by this conversation.

But he didn't seem to resent it. "Well," he hedged with a self-deprecating laugh, "I'd say that yes, I am particularly careful about who I take as far as the bedroom. But has it always been connected to a full-out relationship...? You're right, I am a guy, so—"

"No," she finished for him. "Have you ever lived with a woman?"

He shook his head. "Once I got out on my own I never wanted to share space again. A sleepover, sure. But by morning..." He shrugged. "I'm just the most comfortable on my own," he concluded.

"Have there been women who've tried to change your mind about marriage and kids and domesticity?"

"Sure, there's been a couple who thought they could do that."

"But they couldn't."

He shrugged again.

"Because you are not the marrying kind," she filled in. "I've met a lot of you...."

Just not any who were as forthcoming with that information.

"But you have had long-term relationships in your past—even if you haven't lived with anyone?"

"A few."

Which went back to what she'd originally been wondering—if he might have been hurt, if that was what had really brought him to his no-marriage-ever stance.

"I was with the same person all through college," he went on. "And there have been two relationships since then—one for two years and one for almost three that ended about two years ago."

"Those are reasonably long relationships, and when

things ran their course they just ended?" Vonni asked, trying to grasp that.

"Yeah, basically," he said as if it genuinely hadn't been a big deal.

"No drama? No heartache? No tears?"

He shrugged as if apologizing for not having a juicier story to tell. "When my college girlfriend and I graduated, she went back home to Detroit to go to medical school. Medicine was her dream and she didn't want a husband and family tying her down. She's doing a fellowship in neurosurgery now. We hit it off and had a good time while she was here, but we both knew all along that it had a time limit."

"Plus, it was college, so you were both young," Vonni concluded. She could understand that.

"After Nessa, there was Donna," he continued. "She's a photojournalist and when she started getting regular assignments overseas she took off, and I was happy for her for getting what she wanted."

And again there wasn't the slightest indication that he might have been hurt.

"Then there was Rebecca," he said. "She was a lawyer with visions of sitting on the Supreme Court, so her career came first. Which was okay with me. But somewhere along the way she changed her mind. She decided work wasn't everything, that she did want marriage and kids after all."

"Only she was with you...."

"And she knew where I stood—"

"And just accepted it?"

He made a face that said no. "There was a lot of talking. She was a lawyer, she was used to arguing her case."

"But in the end she couldn't win you over."

"I fixed her up with a friend who'd always had a thing for her," he said as if that should count for something. "I was best man at their wedding in Hawaii last year."

"And you were okay with that?"

"I didn't hand her over as if she was a magazine I'd finished reading. I did some soul-searching about how I'd feel seeing her with Buzzy," he confessed. "But in the end, it couldn't have worked out better for everyone involved."

"And even at their wedding you didn't feel so much as a pang?"

"I was happy for them both. Is that bad?" he asked.

"I don't know," Vonni answered honestly, thinking that he couldn't have had deep feelings for any of the women he'd been in relationships with because if he had, the endings wouldn't have been so cut-and-dried. She wondered if she should feel a little sorry for him for that. But he seemed so content with it all.

"I suppose fixing your ex up with someone else is actually generous. Just weird."

He laughed, and when he did Vonni got lost all over again in how good he looked. "That's pretty much what my family thinks, too, so you're not alone," he said. Then he grinned a slow grin. "But hey, it's better that you think I'm weird than ugly or stupid or smelly or something."

Vonni laughed again. "You're a long way from any of those things...." she said, thinking out loud.

And why had her voice become softer suddenly? Almost inviting...

You're not going to change him any more than you could change the others, a voice in the back of her mind warned her. And she knew it was true.

But she also knew that it was a warm summer night and she was sitting with a gorgeous guy parked in a convertible under the stars. And she felt a little like the teenager she'd once been who might have come here with a guy she liked.

To do exactly what Dane did then, when his hand went from the top of her headrest to her nape and he brought her toward him for a kiss.

A kiss that was identical to the one the night before.

Vonni had relived that kiss a million times in her head since yesterday. But this one managed to be even better, as his lips parted farther and he deepened it.

And while she was aware that she could—and should—put a stop to it, it began to sink in that she just loved kissing him and she couldn't cut that short....

Instead, she raised a hand to the side of his neck and indulged in the feel of his warm skin. She tilted her head a bit more. She let her own lips open. And she kissed him in return with all the abandon of any hormonal, carried-away teen.

Enough abandon to ignite some passion that hadn't been in their previous good-night kiss. Some fire that brought his tongue in search of hers.

His hand massaged its way up into her hair, cradling her head as the kiss settled fully into a make-out session that went on and on, that saw them come up for air only to dive back in, picking up where they'd left off but with even more fervor.

Vonni had no idea how much time passed; she wouldn't have known it if another car had joined them. Nothing existed for her but Dane and his kiss. And what that was stirring up inside of her....

She was very aware of his hand in her hair, of his

other hand brushing the backs of his fingers against her cheek, and she wanted more skin-to-skin action.

She wanted him to pull her shirt out of her waistband, to have his hands on her bare skin. On the bare skin of her back. Her side. Her breasts....

She wanted what could be done in a backseat if only this car had a backseat....

But after her imagination had run away with her, taking her outside of the car to the grassy knoll in front of the car, to lie on the lawn and let everything go so much further, a bit of an alarm finally sounded in her.

They weren't hormonal teenagers.

And this couldn't go any further because there was no chance of a relationship between them.

And because he was still her client! she silently shrieked at herself.

Her tongue retreated and his did, too, but there was still more kissing—playful, sexy, tempting kissing— before she put both hands to his hard chest and pushed ever so slightly, finally pulling away from him to shake her head.

"We have to stop," she said in a voice that lacked conviction. So he merely kissed her again.

"No, really," she said when she'd enjoyed plenty more of that kiss, too, massaging his chest before pushing him away again.

"I know," he agreed reluctantly, laying his forehead on the top of her head. "Why'd you have to go and be such a damn good kisser?"

Vonni smiled at the compliment, which was also a complaint.

"I don't know what happens to me when I'm with you," he said then. "I kind of go to a different place. Out of this world… Out of my head…" He laughed wryly. "Maybe out of my mind."

"Me, too," Vonni whispered.

"It's crazy."

She didn't say so out loud but she felt it, too. She just didn't know why she kept getting so carried away with him.

Then Dane took a deep breath and sat up straight as he exhaled, taking his hands away and letting them plunk onto the steering wheel.

"Home, huh?" he asked as if he was just as reluctant to end the night now as he had been when they'd left the Larimer Lounge.

"My shop," Vonni amended. "That's where my car is."

"Right," he said as if he was working to come out of a fog. "And I'm not going to see you until Friday?" he asked in disbelief as he started the engine, put the top back up and headed for the highway.

That did seem like a long, long time.

But Vonni took herself to task, reminded herself of the realities and said, "Friday."

"When you'll go to the rehearsal dinner with me?"

Oh, that. That was what they'd been talking about, wasn't it….

But before she could say no, he said, "I'm going to drive around until you say yes. GiGi appreciates that you went to the pains you did to do her wedding in a hurry and she wants you there. And I want you there just because I want you there. But if it makes you feel better, let's just say that I want you there out of gratitude, too."

There was no doubt in Vonni's mind that she should stick to her guns and say no. Refuse point-blank, and make sure that from here on she and Dane Camden had absolutely no encounter that involved anything but business, preferably done with his family and her staff all around them.

Of course, his family would be around them at the rehearsal dinner....

The Camden family, who had screwed over her grandfather....

But not even that reminder could make her do what she knew she should do, so there she was, saying yes, she would go to the rehearsal dinner. With him.

Which made him smile at her as if he was thinking that Friday couldn't come soon enough.

Then they were at her shop, in the parking lot behind it and he pulled up beside her car.

"No, just let me get out and go," she said when he reached for his keys to turn off the ignition. She didn't need to get herself into any more trouble tonight.

Vonni left the car in a hurry and closed the door as he lowered the convertible top so he could see her.

"I'll let you know about the caterers and the brunch, and if there are any problems," she said as she unlocked her own car door.

"Or you could just call me for any reason...." he said with what sounded something like hope in his tone.

"Have a good week," was her only answer.

"You, too," he said as if he was conceding to something.

But Vonni counted it as a victory when she got behind the wheel, closed and locked her door and started her own engine, all without having kissed him again.

A huge victory....

That felt like a defeat when what she really wanted was to be back in those arms, being kissed into oblivion all over again.

Chapter Eight

"We weren't sure you were going to make it today."

Dane was playing golf at the country club on Friday afternoon. His grandmother and her fiancé had arrived home from Montana the night before with the eldest of the grandchildren—Dane's cousin, Seth—and Seth's new wife, Lacey. Seth ran the agricultural division of Camden Incorporated from the ranch in Northbridge, Montana.

The women of the family were having massages while the men—minus Gideon Thatcher, Jani's husband—played golf. GiGi's seven grandsons and Jonah Morrison, the groom, were divided into two foursomes. Dane was playing with Seth, Seth's brother Cade, and Dane's younger brother Lang.

"Why wouldn't I have made it today?" Dane responded to Cade's comment.

"You were so interested in watching the wedding planner orchestrating the reception setup we wondered if maybe you were going to hang back and just do that instead. We thought we might have to call Gideon and see if he could take off work after all to round out our numbers."

Dane *had* been watching Vonni pretty intently, he just hadn't realized anyone had noticed. Tuesday, Wednesday and Thursday without her had seemed to drag unbelievably. And not even the brief phone calls to check in had helped because they'd been primarily wedding related and over much more quickly than Dane would have liked.

Then today had finally come and he'd been waiting at GiGi's house for Vonni to arrive to oversee the wedding reception setup. But she'd barely had time to say hello, to be introduced to GiGi and Jonah, before she'd been torn away to work. And that was when Dane had gone upstairs to the second floor to stand at the railing in order to watch her. As unable to take his eyes off her as a starving man in line at a food counter.

"How are things going with getting her on board for the Camdens wedding departments?" Lang asked.

"I'll step that up once GiGi's wedding is under control. So far I've taken a subtle approach," Dane answered. "We had to plan this in such a rush—"

"Oh, yeah," Cade laughed. "I forgot you got that job as your foot in the door to make amends to her family. I don't envy you that one. All I had to do was hire Nati to texture a wall in my house, and Lang got to eat a lot of cheesecake to get to Heddy, but a *wedding?* Glad I didn't get stuck with *that.*"

"Yeah, I was dreading it. But Vonni made it easy," Dane said.

Then he saw the knowing looks his cousin and younger brother exchanged.

"Did she…" Lang said suspiciously.

"She's good at her job, remember?" Dane countered without getting flustered. "That's why this particular act of contrition is to get her to come to work for us setting up wedding departments and running them. We make up to her for buying her grandfather's stolen formulas and in the process get the best wedding planner in town for Camdens—win-win."

"And for you?" Lang goaded.

"For me?" Dane asked as he bent over to position his tee.

"It did look like you were moonin' over that girl," Seth contributed, making himself sound like the country cousin when he didn't ordinarily.

"She's great," Dane said matter-of-factly.

"Is Never Settling Down Dane falling for somebody?" Cade suggested.

Dane took his shot and his brother and two cousins moaned at the sight of a drive so good that it made Dane grin, too.

Only then, calm and collected, did Dane say, "I don't *fall* for anybody because no, I'm not going the marriage-and-family route the way the three of you are."

Cade was engaged, Seth had been married only a few months and Lang was the most recent addition to the married Camdens—he and widow Heddy Hanrahan had gotten married in a small ceremony on June 1 with only family and Lang's three-year-old son, Carter, in attendance.

"Good for you, no thanks for me," Dane concluded as the four of them headed toward the fairway.

"So gawking at her the way you were before we left GiGi's was for business purposes?" Cade asked dubiously.

"I like her," Dane said without compunction. "I told you, she's great."

"Great as more than a wedding planner...." Cade said, continuing to verbally poke at him.

"That's kind of how these missions work, isn't it?" Dane reasoned. "We need to get to know our targets, we want them to get to know us to break through the barrier of whatever problems they have with us from the past and..." Okay, maybe he wasn't quite as cool as he was projecting because then he admitted, "It's tough not to get sucked in. Not to like them if they're likable—"

"It does seem as if they get pretty likable...." Seth said pointedly, referring to the fact that both Lang and Cade had ended up with women they'd set out to make amends to—and Jani had married Gideon Thatcher, another of the people who had been due some compensation for past Camden misdeeds.

"Sure, be smug," Lang said defensively. "You're the one who found H.J.'s journals in Northbridge, and that's what set off this whole need to right the wrongs done in the past. But so far that's all you've had to do—"

"Because when he found the journals he also found Lacey, so GiGi left him alone to concentrate on her," Cade contributed. "You don't know how it is when you're doing these things, Seth—"

"Still, liking the person we're making amends to and ending up with them are two different things," Dane qualified, interrupting all the finger-pointing at Seth. "It's a pleasure doing business with Vonni, but that doesn't mean anything."

"A hot blonde with beautiful green eyes who you were so lost in looking at that I had to nearly body slam you to get your attention?" Seth said. "Right, doesn't sound like anything to me."

"I didn't say she wasn't hot," Dane agreed. "Or that I don't enjoy looking at her. It just doesn't change my own game plan. Now, are we gonna play golf or have tea and crumpets and go on talking like little girls?"

"The way I'm hitting this ball today, tea and crumpets might be a better idea," Cade grumbled as he studied his shot.

Lang and Seth started giving him advice on his golf swing and that put an end to the Vonni talk.

Dane was glad.

But not talking about her still didn't stop him from thinking about her.

And watching her at GiGi's house before he'd left to play golf *had* been particularly engrossing. Because what he'd been thinking about then, and what was still on his mind now, was how much he'd missed her the three days he hadn't seen her. And how, when it came to this woman, he was more confused than he'd been since he'd started noticing girls in the third grade.

He'd been in three relationships that had lasted years. He'd dated other women for weeks or months. And not once had he experienced what he was experiencing with Vonni.

Nothing kept him from thinking about her.

It was the strangest thing.

And on top of it, those few days without her had had him feeling completely off-kilter and he hadn't understood *that,* either. He'd actually wondered if he was coming down with something.

Then today, one look at her, being with her, and everything had gone right again. Back in balance. And he couldn't have felt better. Especially knowing he was going to get to be with her tonight. Knowing he'd see her again tomorrow. Knowing there weren't any Vonni voids on the immediate horizon. It left him feeling the way he had as a kid the day after Halloween with a hoard of candy.

It was all very peculiar.

And then there was the kissing....

That was something else he couldn't explain.

Regardless of how attracted he might have been to any other women, if they were out of bounds he'd managed to have some restraint. And he'd never—ever—crossed the line with someone he worked with.

But Vonni was doubly out of bounds and yet all it took was a little time with her, a little looking into those green eyes of hers, a little talking to her and he couldn't stop himself.

Why was that? he wondered as he watched Cade take a swing.

But he didn't know why. He just knew he needed to figure it out.

To fix it....

Although...

As he stood back to watch Seth take his turn, it occurred to Dane that as the guy who got the impossible done when it came to business, he had to know when to push, when to fix something and when to just have some patience. When to leave things alone and allow them to run their course.

And maybe this was one of those things.

Since what was happening with Vonni had never happened with any other woman, it was likely just a fluke and it would run *its* course and resolve itself.

And if it didn't, *then* he could work on finding a fix—the way he did in business.

The more he thought about it, the better he liked that idea.

For now it was just so nice to be back in the groove of seeing Vonni again that he didn't want to use that time to analyze anything. He just wanted to drink it in and rehydrate after the three-day drought without her.

Plus, the whole family was together, GiGi was getting married and it was a weekend for celebrating—it seemed like he should have a few days' free pass. Especially after being the one to plan his grandmother's wedding. He could think of it as his reward.

So maybe he'd give it that long a course—a few days wasn't any big deal. And if by Monday he wasn't back to normal then he'd try to figure things out.

But for now he was just going to enjoy himself.

Postwedding, postweekend, postcelebration, he'd get on with trying to convince Vonni to come to work for Camdens, he'd devote himself to business and possibly by then everything would be back to normal on its own.

It could happen.

And if it did, then there might not even be anything *to* figure out.

Keeping in mind, of course, that in the meantime he couldn't let things go too far because the goal was ultimately to have Vonni working for Camdens and he needed not to do anything to screw that up.

Which he swore he wouldn't do.

But for now, there was just the wedding to focus on.

With Vonni in the mix.

And he wasn't going to think any more about why that gave him as much of a boost as it did....

Vonni ended up attending the wedding rehearsal for Georgianna Camden's wedding on Friday evening.

During the course of the prewedding-day setup and meeting the bride and groom and the rest of the Camdens, Georgianna Camden had asked Vonni's opinion on some elements of the ceremony itself—the bride wanted the private part to be relaxed but she also wanted it to be momentous and gracious and decorous.

Vonni had offered a few suggestions and in the process she'd been asked by the matriarch of the Camden family if she would come to the rehearsal and tell them all what to do for that, too.

The Camdens, Margaret and Louie Haliburton and the judge performing the ceremony were as amenable as Dane had been during the planning stages. They made it easy for her to tell them all what to do. So she helped stage manage that, as well.

But as Vonni went through the rehearsal and then the dinner outside on the patio, she found it difficult not to like the Camdens. They were clearly a close-knit family. But even to the outsiders of the gathering—Vonni included—they were warm, friendly people, a modest, unassuming, humble bunch. Just like Dane. They were unlike many of Chrystal's upper-crust friends and Vonni's other clients, who tended to be entitled, demanding and difficult.

But the Camdens were also descendants of people who had been so unscrupulous that they'd bought her grandfather's stolen formulas without regard to anything but getting what they'd wanted. That was something she kept reminding herself even during the most enjoyable parts of the evening and as the Camdens' job offer continued to float around the peripheries of her mind.

"Okay, this is the last trip for the baskets, the envelopes with the checks in them are right by the front door so you can take them with you when you leave and now we can relax and have our pie," Dane said as he and Vonni brought the final two gift baskets into his condominium after the rehearsal dinner.

He'd volunteered for the job of delivering the gift baskets that she'd assembled during the week. They were going to the hotel where the out-of-town guests would be staying and needed to be there first thing in the morning in order to be placed in the rooms before the guests arrived.

Vonni also needed to pick up the checks she would be distributing to her vendors. Dane had forgotten to bring them to his grandmother's house, so she'd followed him from the Camden family home to his two-story stucco condo just off Josephine Street.

He'd parked in his garage around back while Vonni had parked at the curb in front, just outside of the walled-in courtyard. He'd told her to wait in her car until he came through the town house to open the front door.

She didn't wait long, but it had been long enough for her to assess the very-high-end row houses that took up a full block in the country club neighborhood. They were a contemporary southwestern style that was sophisticated and chic, but didn't strike Vonni as inviting to family or pets.

She had the same impression when she went inside Dane's particular condo—it was impeccably decorated in very angular modern Scandinavian furniture with several sculptures on pillars that would be at risk with a dog or kids running around.

"Fancy place," she commented when he closed the door behind them.

"Is it?" he asked as if it didn't strike him as that. "I know it has a different feel to it than what we looked at for you, but fancy?"

To Vonni it had a museum feel to it, but she didn't want to say that, so she stuck with fancy and added, "It's beautiful," because it was. There just wasn't any warmth to it, unlike Dane himself.

"What about your place?" he asked then. "Have you heard anything on your offer?"

"The seller accepted it, but the house has to be inspected before the deal goes any further."

The brick cottage with its front porch, its big backyard, and its homey feel inside and out was nothing at all like this place. This place could have come straight off the pages of an architecture-and-interior-design magazine. But she still couldn't imagine actually living in it.

"Pie in the living room or the kitchen?" he asked then.

Margaret's gourmet rehearsal dinner had left them too full for dessert, but both Margaret and Dane's grandmother had insisted that they take slices of the apple pie with them.

Vonni had been hesitant about following Dane to his place tonight. After three days of not seeing him and only talking to him on the phone about wedding things, she was well aware that she should continue the more professional tone that they'd set. Despite having just spent the evening dining with his family as if she were one of them, when it came to Dane she should maintain the distance that the three-day break had provided.

So now that she'd accomplished the business she'd come for, she knew that she shouldn't stick around to eat her slice of pie. That she should take it and go.

But suddenly even that absolute certainty didn't carry any weight.

She'd missed him so horribly the past three days that she was at the mercy of those feelings. And even having seen him at his grandmother's house earlier in the day and again tonight hadn't helped. There had been so much going on and so many other people around, that it hadn't felt as if she was *with* him.

It had been *three* days. Three days that had seemed like three years. And she needed just a little of him...

"Your house, your rules," she said in answer to his inquiry about whether they should have pie in the kitchen or the living room, telling herself that it *was* only pie after all. Harmless pie that wouldn't take long to eat and then she'd go.

"Living room," he decided.

Vonni was wearing a red wraparound dress tied at her waist, with four-inch spike heels that matched. Her shoes made a hollow-sounding *clack-clack-clack* on his hardwood floors as they took their plates into the stark living room.

There were square white leather cubes to sit on or a long black leather-and-chrome sofa, so she opted for the sofa, sitting not quite at one end but not quite in the middle, either.

Dane joined her there, sitting smack-dab in the center so that he wasn't far from her.

He'd been wearing a dark blue suit during the rehearsal and dinner but had since shucked the coat and tie, unfastened the collar button of his pale blue shirt and rolled his sleeves to his forearms.

And he just looked so good....

"So what did you think of us?" he asked bluntly after Vonni had tasted the pie and rhapsodized about how good it was. "Think we'd be all right to work with? Or did you think that you wouldn't be able to stand it?"

"Everyone was very nice," she said truthfully. "I can't imagine anyone *not* liking your grandmother—she's so friendly and she was appreciative of everything we planned for the wedding. She gave me so many compliments my head started to swell. And every one of your brothers and sisters and cousins said they hoped I'd come on board with Camden Superstores." But she hadn't felt as if she'd been on one giant interview, which had been a pleasant surprise. "They all made me feel like visiting royalty rather than the plain old wedding planner or someone they were thinking about hiring."

"Want to sign on the dotted line here and now?" he asked buoyantly.

Vonni laughed. "Really? It's almost eleven o'clock on a Friday night and we're having *pie*.... Do you really want to talk business?"

"I do if it means you'll say yes to heading up Camdens' wedding departments."

But that wasn't her answer. The Camdens had been far more friendly than most of her clients and not at all daunting, but there was still a sour history there, and she remained on the fence about the job offer. Or, actually, just standing *at* the fence because while she was concerned with what wedding departments at Camden Superstores would do to her friend's business, she continued to prefer the idea of the promised partnership that would turn Burke's Weddings into Burke and Hunter Weddings.

So what she said was, "I loved Jonah, too—what a sweetheart."

Dane smiled. "So maybe not a no on coming to work with us but not a yes yet, either. Okay, I get it," he conceded. "Let's talk about something else.... Jonah—he's a great guy. He's good for GiGi, he makes her happy. So don't get any idea about stealing him."

Vonni laughed. "Too late, I've already thought about it, tried and been shot down."

Dane smiled again but this time it was more inquisitive. "I just realized that I've never asked about your own marital status.... By now it's pretty clear there's no husband, but how is it that the wedding planner isn't married herself? Or have you been and it didn't work out and it's a sore subject?"

"I've never been married. But not for want of trying," she said, laughing again.

"Ah, so there *have* been other grooms like Jonah who you've made a play for...."

"I've been dumb when it comes to men, but not *that* dumb."

"Dumb? You? I don't believe that. You told me you were smart enough in school to stay away from guys you knew wouldn't end up taking you home to meet the parents, and now you're telling me something changed when you got out of school to make you dumb about dating?"

"I've been misled more than I let myself be in school, and I'm beginning to feel kind of dumb, yeah. That's part of why I'm taking time off from dating and regrouping."

His eyebrows arched. "You said you've met a lot of guys who are not the marrying kind. Have they jerked you around?"

He sounded as if he wanted to go out and defend her honor, and that made her smile. "They've strung me along," she amended. "I give you credit for letting women know right from the start that you aren't interested in marriage. I've run into too many who either say they are and aren't, or say they are, they're just not ready yet, and then never get ready. Or there was the last one—when he *was* ready he went back to an old girlfriend."

"No? Seriously?"

"Seriously," she confirmed.

"Are we talking long-term or short-term stringing you along?"

"Three that were long-term—just like you. But there have been too many that go on for a few months—sometimes six—before I figure out that it isn't going where I want it to."

"But the three long-term were the worst...."

"Sure. Two of them cost me four and a half years between them, and the third cost me almost three years all on its own."

"Was the guy who went back to an old girlfriend around for almost three years before he did that?"

"That was the one."

"And the other two just pretended they wanted to get married but it never panned out?"

"The first guy, Tanner, kept saying he *did* want to get married, but not before we were both twenty-five—"

"Then you hit twenty-five and no deal?"

"We hit twenty-five after over two years together, and when I pushed, he bailed."

"And the second?"

"David. I was with him for just under two years, thinking that he was going to propose because when I'd talk about marriage he would agree that it had a lot to recommend it and he'd make some reference to our being together in the future. Just under two years of thinking maybe he would propose on my birthday, or on his birthday, or maybe for Valentine's Day. Thinking he might propose on the next vacation, the anniversary of our first date, his parents' anniversary, two Christmases, two New Years—"

"That's a lot of disappointed hopes."

"A lot," she agreed. "Only to have him shrug when

I asked when it *was* going to happen, and say he just couldn't commit."

"And that led to the guy who went back to an old girlfriend?"

"Mark." Her voice had begun to echo with the pain that had accompanied all of her romantic defeats and Dane apparently heard it, because rather than asking for details, he said, "So you've been kind of bruised up and you need some time off from dating to heal."

"I've been bruised, yes, but it isn't only that I need time off to heal. I've also put my whole life on hold waiting to have a husband—as if life wouldn't begin until that happened—and I'm not doing that anymore. I'm taking a hiatus from the husband hunt and—"

"Buying a house and getting a dog—that's what you've waited for," he concluded insightfully.

"Yes," she confirmed.

"Soo…taking a hiatus from the husband hunt…. *Have* you been *hunting?*"

Regardless of the fact that being with Dane always felt like a date, Vonni was not in dating mode when she was with him, and she liked that. She liked that there had never been any coyness between them, that there hadn't been any game playing, any of the dating ritual or the subterfuge. She liked that they could just talk openly.

"It may be hard for you to understand—given your own mind-set—but I *do* want to get married. To have kids. A family. Someone to go home to at night, someone who's there for me. And I've put a lot of effort into trying to find that someone."

"You weren't kidding about the dating profiles?" he said, referring to the slip of the tongue she'd made last week in response to a compliment he'd given her.

But then, she hadn't wanted to reveal too much and she considered whether or not to now.

She'd come this far, though, and thought why not. He'd been honest with her about what he wanted and didn't want; why shouldn't she be honest with him?

"After trying all the usual routes to just meet someone—"

"Bars and clubs and friends of friends, and brothers of friends, and blind dates?" he guessed.

"Right—after all of that, I decided to go the more organized route...."

"Organized?" he echoed, taking her empty dessert dish and setting it down with his on the rectangular glass box that served as his coffee table.

Then he resettled himself by angling more in her direction and propping an elbow on the top of the sofa back before he said, "First of all, the same way I find it hard to believe that every guy you ever went to school with didn't jump through hoops to have you, I find it even more hard to believe that you've had *any* trouble finding someone to marry if that's what you want. And I admire you for not letting your parents' unhappy marriage scare you from wanting marriage yourself—"

"Because I told you I want to believe that it's possible for two people to find each other, make a life together and live happily ever after."

"But it isn't just that you *want to believe* that—you're actively beating the bushes for it?"

"I have been...."

She readjusted a little, too, turning more toward him on the slippery leather couch so they were facing each other. When she did that, her thigh came through the split where the two ends of the wrap dress's skirt draped together and she had to cover it.

Which caught Dane's attention, but he raised his gaze

from her thigh after a split-second's ogle and looked at her face again.

"So what have you done?" he asked.

"Pretty much everything," Vonni admitted with a laugh at herself. "I've tried dating sites on the internet, and groups in town, and meet-a-mate events, and the just-lunch thing, and one that sends you a message on your phone if you're in the same vicinity as someone else who belongs. I've done speed dating, and mixers, and I even went to a matchmaker…."

"You're *serious* serious…." he said, sounding truly surprised.

She shrugged. "It's what I want and when it wasn't happening naturally, I decided to do it like any other project—to dedicate myself to it."

"And is that what you'll do again—after your hiatus?"

"Probably," she said frankly. "But whatever I do, I know I'm going to go at it differently—"

"How so?"

"I guess it isn't just the guys—I haven't been as up-front as you are, either. It's supposed to be bad form to say from the get-go that you're in the market for a husband, that you want kids and a house and dog and the whole package. You're supposed to play it cool so you don't scare the guy off. You're supposed to let them pursue you. Ease them into the idea of marriage and family by showing how domestic you can be, by hanging out with happily married couples—"

"Is there a handbook out there somewhere?"

"Many—there are self-help books for women, women's magazines, talk shows aimed at women, mothers…. It's the advice women are given. And I've followed it—"

"But you aren't going to when you go back on the hunt?"

"No. I'm going your route—I'm going to let it be known right out of the gate that I want marriage and a family. And if that isn't what the guy wants—and wants right away—then that's it, no second wink or second coffee or lunch or dinner or whatever it is that starts things off. Either we're looking for the same thing or we aren't, and if we aren't, then I'm not wasting my time."

His grin came slowly, as if she was amusing him, but only in the nicest way. And just the sight of that handsome face erupting into an approving expression gave her goose bumps.

Goose bumps that she tried to ignore.

"I like it," he decreed as if she was selling him on something. "In the first place, I don't think you should have to put what you want on hold for any reason—you should have a house if you want a house, and you should definitely have One-Eyed Charlie the dog if you want One-Eyed Charlie the dog. And I agree with being up front—why should there be any illusions or false hopes? There's nothing wrong with wanting what you want and going after it, and not wasting time on anybody who isn't on the same page. Or the same timeline."

"That's what I've decided," she concluded, having no idea why it pleased her to have his sanction.

Or why it was so easy to get lost in the smile that went with it....

For a moment neither of them said anything and it didn't seem to matter. It didn't even seem the slightest bit awkward that they were sitting there just looking at each other.

Then, in a quiet voice, Dane said, "You really are one of a kind and I missed you *fiercely* the past three days."

Vonni didn't want to admit the same thing so she joked, "Should I add *fiercely* missable to my dating profile when I get out there again?"

"Hmm," he muttered with a tiny frown creasing his brow. "Why don't I want to think about you *getting out there again* right now?"

She had no answer to that. But he reached around to clasp her nape then, moving them both into a kiss that made it unnecessary and impossible to say anything, anyway.

Vonni had missed him, too, but even though she'd thought that she'd missed him intensely, she realized only when his mouth took hers just how much she'd longed for him. For this, as well as his company. It really was as if kissing him was something vital to her that she'd been without, and in that moment she could only let herself have the sustenance of it. She could only give herself over to it and let it restore her.

His kiss was so wonderfully familiar by then that it seemed completely natural that her lips parted in answer to his, that their tongues met and toyed with each other, that Dane's arm went around her and pulled her closer and her hands rose so her palms could lie flat against his chest.

Familiar and natural and then more as their mouths widened and that kiss found a new level. A new, intense level...

Dane's hand slid from her neck down her shoulder, down her arm, jumping off the cliff of her elbow to her side, her hip and then to that thigh that had peeked from the split in her skirt earlier.

Had he been thinking about doing this ever since?

She thought it was possible as he massaged and caressed her thigh.

And it did feel great. His hand was big and warm and strong and those long fingers pressed into her flesh just enough.

Just enough to make other parts of her come awake and crave the same thing—that hand, that caress, that massage. Only it was her breasts that were suddenly calling out for the attention.

Vonni's own hands coursed up to his shoulders and over them to his broad back, learning the hills and valleys through his shirt and wishing she could slip her fingers underneath the fabric.

Driven by the need for more of the feel of skin to skin, she tugged his shirttails free of his slacks and found the hot silk of flesh over honed muscle.

It had an impact because the kissing went up another notch to erotic and that hand at her thigh climbed just a little higher, turning Vonni on that much more before he eased it over her skirt and up to her breast.

This time it was Vonni who contributed a hint more fervor to the kissing as her own hands took firmer hold of his back and the faintest sigh came out just short of a moan.

She hadn't planned the wrap dress for this but she was only too happy when it accommodated his hand slipping inside to the lacy demi-cup of her bra.

Now, if only the bra would disappear....

It didn't actually have to, though, because Dane was dexterous and insinuated his hand between lace and breast, taking the breast into his palm where her nipple became a tiny pebble to let him know how good it felt.

And then how much better when he began that same massage he'd done at her thigh.

It felt so good that Vonni's spine arched, giving him more access and a freer rein. One hand came out from under his shirt—also to open the way—but when she rested it on his upper thigh she realized only belatedly that it was perilously close to a bulge in his lap.

Close enough to feel him growing against the back of her thumb.

She could have moved her hand. But instead she raised her bare thigh to rest it on top of his and her mind began to strip him out of those clothes he had on and picture him naked....

Naked...

While a portion of her mind imagined the glory of that, another portion began to wonder about other things.

Like what she was doing!

They weren't in dating mode—they weren't dating! She'd just been thinking earlier about how that was a good thing. But how did they keep ending up kissing?

It certainly didn't go along with being her client.

It didn't go along with her being on hiatus from the husband hunt.

It didn't go along with him being antimarriage and not wanting a family for himself.

So what was she doing? she asked herself.

And she wasn't even *only* kissing him!

Oh, but it felt so good....

He was flicking her nipple with a feathery fingertip, then squeezing it just gently. Squeezing and rolling and then kneading her entire breast again, and it was all just about driving her out of her mind....

But not so far out of her mind—yet—that rational thought didn't intrude and remind her that she needed to put a stop to this because of the client/husband-hunting-hiatus/no-marriage-ever things.

In just a minute...

No, now! That rational thought shouted at her because even just a minute more and that part of her knew she was going to be lost.

So she did draw the hand in his lap away. She did pull out her other hand from inside of Dane's shirt, and she put them both on his chest again, leveraging herself backward, away from him. From that kiss. And from that so, so talented hand that fell away from her breast....

"Probably not the best idea...." she said in a voice that was ragged and rueful enough to convey how much she didn't want to stop.

He nodded without agreeing and tugged the edge of her dress back into place with his index and middle finger.

Vonni sat up straighter and did a better job of it, also closing the split in her skirt while he said, "There's just something about—"

"I know," she confirmed, not knowing how he was going to finish the sentence but understanding that there *was* just something about the two of them together that led to things going where they had no business going.

Then she decided that business was the best refuge so she stood and said, "I have an 11:00 a.m. wedding tomorrow with a lunch reception. Once that's going on its own speed I'll leave and come to your grandmother's house. We couldn't set up in the kitchen today because of tonight's dinner, and there's more that needs to be done out on the patio, so those will be where we concentrate our efforts before the ceremony. But everything should be up and running by the time the judge has done the honors and you're all ready to receive guests."

He'd walked her to the door by then, and she took

the envelopes as he said, "I'm sure you've got everything under control."

Everything but what was still charging through her that made her want to kiss him again.

And put his hand back on her breasts.

And rip those clothes off him after all....

But she reined in those thoughts, those inclinations, and pretended she wasn't having them at all as he walked her out to her car.

Only there—once she'd unlocked and opened her door—he pulled her into his arms and kissed her again very soundly, as if to let her know he hadn't forgotten about any of what had just happened even if she was pretending she had.

Then he let go of her, grasped the top of her door in one hand and laid the other on the roof of her sedan while she got behind the wheel.

"I'll see you tomorrow," he said then.

"Tomorrow afternoon," she added just before he closed her door.

But as she drove off, stealing glances of him watching her go in her rearview mirror, she had the distinct impression that she'd left him in the same frame of mind and body that she was in.

And there was nothing at all final about it.

Instead, she just wanted him even more than she had before....

Chapter Nine

"Dane Camden, this is Chrystal Burke."

Vonni performed the introduction her friend asked her to make when Chrystal arrived half an hour after the Camden wedding reception began.

Chrystal had already introduced herself to the bride and groom, and as usual was acting as if she'd had something to do with the wedding itself. Now Vonni, Chrystal and Dane were in the dining room where Vonni had just made sure the hors d'oeuvre trays were being taken out by the waitstaff to be offered to the guests.

Vonni looked on as Dane made small talk with Chrystal and pointedly told her how much he and his family appreciated all that *Vonni* had done and the great lengths *Vonni* had gone to in order to have this wedding on short notice.

Vonni knew that his efforts on her behalf were wasted on Chrystal, but she appreciated them nonetheless and merely stood by and enjoyed the sight of him.

For the wedding he was dressed in an almost-black suit. Under the coat he was wearing a white shirt striped with silver-white lines, and a matching white silk tie with those barely-visible white lines on the diagonal in the tie.

She'd never seen clothes fit any man better than these fit him, and her first glimpse of him coming out of the den after the wedding ceremony had nearly made her jaw drop. Add to it his clean-shaven chiseled features and the artfully careless hair and he was the biggest distraction she'd ever experienced at a wedding.

But she still needed to do her job, she reminded herself.

"I should check and make sure dinner is going to be on time," she said in the midst of Chrystal flirting with Dane. "But, Chrystal, could we find a minute later to talk?"

"You know what?" Dane said as if she'd given him an opening. "I'm going to leave you ladies to talk right now because I can see one of my brothers needing to be rescued. If you two will excuse me." Then he grasped Vonni's elbow lightly, leaned close to her ear and said, "I'll catch up with you later," and left.

"Ooh…" Chrystal said in a singsong once he was gone. "That looked interesting. Is something going on between you after all?"

"We just did the wedding together," Vonni answered, not wanting to admit to her friend what she didn't want to admit to herself—that yes, *something* was going on no matter how she fought it, and that she didn't know exactly what it was.

But she really had wanted to talk to Chrystal, so now that she had the opportunity she got to the point.

"I never heard back from you about having lunch with your dad."

Chrystal made a face of dread. "He can't have lunch. He's involved with some big merger. He wouldn't even have dinner with me until last night. But…I do need to talk to you…. It's the main reason I came today."

There was nothing positive in Chrystal's tone and it wasn't like her to stammer, so Vonni had to assume that her friend wasn't eager to say what she had to say. "He's putting off the partnership again," Vonni guessed.

"I'm sorry, Vonni," Chrystal said, sounding genuinely remorseful. "I tried. I really did. But that's not the worst of it…."

"There's something worse?"

"You know Daddy's new girlfriend—*Gina?*" Chrystal said the name with scorn. "Well, now she's his fiancée…. They're getting married. She's already moved into the house and…she wants to work at Burke's Weddings."

"Doing what?" Vonni asked cautiously, trying not to jump to any ominous conclusions.

"Daddy wants you to show her the ropes so she can do everything you do and be a-a second coordinator…."

"A second coordinator," Vonni repeated. "So she won't be working *for* me—for us," she amended in order to maintain the illusion that Chrystal had any real part in the shop. "She'll be equal?"

Chrystal shrugged and actually looked a little beaten. "Equal for now…."

"Are you telling me she's going to take over? I'm supposed to teach someone how to do everything I do so she can take my job?"

"Daddy is marrying her, Vonni, and you know how it is…. Burke's Weddings is technically Daddy's business, so he's really the one who has the say in what goes on—"

"And he's going to take away your graduation gift and make it a wedding gift for his new bride?"

Chrystal shrugged again and didn't look any too happy. "He told me this over dinner the other night and it actually got kind of…unpleasant. I said we didn't need anyone else to work at Burke's Weddings and he made fun of my saying *we*. He made a really ugly remark about it, and said if he'd given me a car I didn't drive he'd have the right to take that back, too, and that Gina is so wonderful and so stylish and has such good taste—"

Chrystal's voice cracked and Vonni saw tears well in her friend's eyes. But she was so mired in her own shock and worry that she didn't know what to say and merely reached out and rubbed Chrystal's arm comfortingly.

"He said that right now there's no Burke in Burke's Weddings and that's my fault. That when Gina becomes Mrs. Burke there will be. It was all just so…*ugly*…. He thinks the sun rises and sets on *Gina*—it's like she has him brainwashed—and I'm just… I don't know, nothing good. I don't work, I wasted his money on a college education, I left my graduation-gift business to be run by you while I just have my hair and nails done and shop all the time—that's what he said. I had no idea he thought I was so useless, but he even said that…."

Vonni swallowed back her own anxiety when Chrystal turned away to face the dining room table rather than the guests and dabbed an index finger under her eye to catch the tear that fell before it could harm her makeup.

"I'm sorry, Chrystal."

"I'm sorry, too. I know what you've put into Burke's

Weddings and now Daddy could let *Gina* just swoop in and take it away from both of us."

But despite the fact that it might be a personal blow to Chrystal, it wouldn't change anything for her. For Vonni the world seemed to be suddenly spinning out of control.

"I suppose we can hope that *Gina* will be like me," Chrystal said then. "Maybe she'll work for a while then just want to spend more time being a wife and things will go back to being the way they are...."

Even if that happened—and Vonni knew she couldn't bank on it—Vonni still wouldn't be a partner.

But she wouldn't contribute to her friend's misery by venting her own anger and frustration, so she didn't say that.

"In the meantime," she said instead, "when is Gina coming into the picture?"

"Monday."

"Monday. *This* Monday? The day after tomorrow?" Chrystal nodded.

"So not a lot of warning," Vonni muttered.

"He said *poor Gina* is bored because he's so busy with the merger and he wants her to get started so she has something to do. I fought for us, Vonni. For both of us. I said he's been promising you the partnership for *years* and now instead of that he's giving you *Gina,* but there's no getting through to him."

Vonni nodded, not doubting that Chrystal had gone to bat for her to whatever degree she could.

"Well..." she said, trying to gather her wits. "I'm in the middle of a wedding and there's nothing I can do about this right now."

"I'm not going to stay," Chrystal said. "I just wanted to meet the Camdens and see the inside of the house, and tell you what's happened...." Chrystal nodded in the direction of Dane then and said, "I hope something *is* going on with him—you deserve that, at least. I'll come in Monday to introduce you to *Gina*." Then, looking forlorn and dejected, she added, "I'm so sorry, Vonni."

Vonni merely nodded and watched Chrystal make her way past the guests before being stopped by someone who knew her on her way to the front door.

There were things that Vonni needed to check on, but at that moment all she could do was stand there, stunned.

No partnership. After eight years of building Burke's Weddings, she was still nothing more than an employee and never would be....

This was no better than the failed relationships she'd let herself be strung along through, hoping that what she wanted would manifest itself naturally, that if she worked hard enough and wanted it enough and proved herself, it would surely come to her....

Except that no marriage proposal ever had.

And now neither had her partnership....

"Hey! You look like something hit you. Are you okay?"

Dane.

Vonni had been so lost in her own thoughts that she hadn't even seen him coming.

"I looked up from hearing about weather patterns in Northbridge," he was saying, "and you were just standing here with the color gone from your face."

Vonni blinked as if she was coming out of a coma, took a deep breath and said, "I think maybe we should talk about the job you offered me."

"Okay. Great," Dane said with confusion in his voice.

"Now isn't the best time, though. How about after the wedding? We'll go back to my place, I'll pour you a stiff drink—because you look like you could use one—and we can talk all you want about it."

Vonni nodded, still too shocked to worry about the logistics of his suggestion or whether or not she should go to his condo again, especially after last night.

"Can I take over whatever you need to do here, now?" he offered. "Maybe you can go outside and get some air?"

Vonni laughed, thinking that apparently everyone thought what she did was easy. But she knew he was just trying to help. The way he had numerous times since they'd met. And she appreciated that.

"No, I'm okay. I'll take care of everything. I want this to be nice for your grandmother."

"And then we'll talk when it's over," he reiterated reassuringly.

"Good. Yeah. We'll talk later," she said quietly, thinking that this was probably how her grandfather had felt when he'd gone to his safe and found the formulas for his makeup missing.

And how ironic it was that now she was looking to a Camden to solve her problem....

"I keep asking myself if this is sleeping with the enemy.... Well, you know, not *sleeping* but consorting...."

Vonni was still in somewhat of a daze even hours after Chrystal had dropped the bomb on her. She'd seen the Camden wedding reception through to the end, making sure the house was back in order, all the vendors had been paid, tipped and had left and that everything was prepped for the next day's brunch, before she'd considered her job done. Then she had once again followed Dane back to his condominium, where she'd told him the news that had been delivered to her earlier.

They were in his state-of-the-art kitchen where he'd poured them each a glass of the finest scotch Vonni had ever tasted.

But that was basically the end of the line for her.

After accepting the glass she'd wilted against the edge of one of the counters, stepping out of her shoes without really thinking about it. She'd been so absorbed in her problems that she'd barely noticed that the ice in her glass had caused some condensation to form, and a drop of moisture to fall onto the tight, short skirt of her sleeveless navy blue cowl-necked dress. She just didn't care.

Dane seemed to have realized she'd gone as far as she could go at that point because with his own glass in hand, he'd leaned against the opposite counter's edge, facing her. And there they'd stayed, in the kitchen, talking thoroughly and more seriously than ever before about her going to work for Camden Superstores.

"I promise you, I'm not the enemy," he assured her.

He also hadn't said "I told you so" when she'd ranted about Chrystal's father not only refusing her the partnership but having so little regard for her that he would expect her to teach his fiancée how to be a wedding planner so she could be handed the business Vonni had built. She appreciated that.

"What we're offering is better than a partnership in a small shop," he said.

"But I won't be doing any actual weddings myself?"

"Once everything is up and running, that will be up to you. If you want, your personal services and attention can be requested, and you can pick and choose which weddings you want to do yourself—that could even be what attracts high-society weddings to us rather than to shops like Burke's Weddings."

Vonni was sipping her scotch and she smiled weakly at that notion. "You think I'm a big-enough name to bring couples in?"

"I do," he said unequivocally. "In Denver, for now. But once customers from all over see weddings you've put together, yeah, I think people are going to start asking for you to do their individual weddings. And the reason the deal is better even than a partnership in a small shop is that we'll give you a contract that will provide more stability and genuine security than you have now or would have as a partner in Burke's Weddings. Howard Burke is always going to keep a controlling interest, and that means that what he's doing now, he could do even if you were a partner because he'd still have the ultimate say in running things. Plus small shops can go under in the blink of an eye, and that isn't going to happen with us."

He smiled roguishly and added, "Not to mention that we'll pay you enough to buy three of the houses you have an offer on now and keep your animal shelter in dog food forever."

Vonni liked that he was injecting some humor into what was very much a business discussion. It helped lift her spirits. But she was still leery of going to work for the Camdens.

"Would I be crazy to do this?" she said, thinking out loud. "Your family helped cheat my grandfather. Should I really go to work for you and hand over all my ideas and designs and experience?"

Dane didn't respond to that, not even to deny her accusation. Instead, he opened a drawer near the sink, took out paper and pencil and wrote something. Then he handed the paper to her.

"That's the name of a great attorney who hates us. *Hates* us, Vonni. He'll nail us to the wall if he gets the chance. Hire him to hammer out a contract that doesn't leave you in any kind of jeopardy. That protects you in every eventuality. That doesn't have a loophole even a gnat could go through. And that—if for any reason you ever part ways with Camdens—provides you with enough severance to start your own business."

"Should you be giving me advice like that?" she asked.

"You're worth it."

He was looking into her eyes when he said that and while everything else so far had been businesslike, there was something about that look that wasn't.

She was already feeling particularly weak willed. She'd taken a body blow tonight. She'd had her entire future snatched right from under her nose. And here he was, tall and gorgeous and sweet and understanding and offering what seemed like the opportunity of a lifetime. So for him to take things to a personal level at that moment was even more heady than the scotch. The scotch that was going into her nearly empty stomach and certainly not helping strengthen her will to resist anything.

"And you'd be my boss...."

He smiled and shook his head. "If you're asking if we'll be working together, the answer is no. *You'll* be the head of the wedding division, and I'm usually dealing with the big picture of new store development and expansion—getting the impossible done, remember? Our paths probably won't even cross except maybe by accident—so if you're hoping to be finished with me because you can't stand the sight of me, you're in luck."

She hadn't done very well with that in the three days they'd been apart. But it *was* probably better if they wouldn't be working together because she really needed to shut down the things he was stirring in her, to get on with her life, to finish regrouping and recharging, and then go back to her pursuit of a husband when she was ready. And none of that was likely to happen if they continued to spend any amount of time together.

After tonight...

"You are pretty hard to look at," she teased him, realizing only then that somewhere along the way he'd removed all but his shirt and slacks.

"But I will be working for you...." she said, thinking that while she shouldn't have let things happen between them when he'd been her client, she certainly shouldn't let anything happen between herself and one of the people who owned the company she worked for.

If she took the job....

Dane nodded slowly, his eyes never leaving hers. "Technically, if you work for Camden Incorporated, you do work for the Camdens, and I'm a Camden." Then he paused for a moment and she saw something change in him. Switch gears. And he wasn't Business Dane anymore. He was the Dane she'd planned his grandmother's wedding with.

The Dane she was so, so susceptible to....

"But you aren't working for me right now...." he finally added.

Hmm...

Somewhere in the back of Vonni's mind she knew that she might be playing with fire or tempting fate or something along those lines. But at that moment she didn't care about that any more than she cared about the drop of water on her skirt. She just wanted to block out everything else for a little while. And follow nothing but her instincts.

And her instincts were screaming for her to just get herself into the arms of the man she'd planned the wedding with. The man who had a reputation for making women feel better....

She kept her gaze trained on him as she finished her scotch and set her glass on the counter behind her.

"Right now," she heard herself volley coyly, "you aren't my client anymore, either...."

"No, I'm not your client anymore," he confirmed, doing the same with his glass. "Right now you're just you, and I'm just me...." There was another pause before he smiled with only one side of that supple mouth of his and said, "Could that be a window of opportunity?"

A window of opportunity.

But not a door opening to something more between them because they didn't want the same things, Vonni thought.

Only maybe tonight that was okay. Maybe tonight that was actually exactly what she needed.

It seemed as if they were in a sort of limbo between so many things. And while she'd thought before that being on holiday from her quest for a husband meant she was taking a break from men in general, it occurred to her then that that didn't need to be the case. That a moratorium on husband hunting didn't necessarily mean a moratorium on men in general. And if that was true, what better man to find some much-needed solace with tonight than someone she already knew was absolutely not a potential mate?

Chrystal had made that point when her friend had first heard that Vonni would be working with Dane.

Chrystal had encouraged her to have a *rejuvenating* fling with him *because* he wasn't husband material.

And suddenly Vonni decided she agreed with her friend. Wholeheartedly...

"A window of opportunity," she repeated in a voice that was breathier than it had been. "We're not talking about a job anymore, are we?"

He laughed. "I'm not," he confessed. "But I can start again if you want me to."

She thought about that, gave herself the opportunity to stop before anything got started.

But she just didn't want to. Not tonight.

So she pushed away from the counter's edge and took a step closer to him. "No, thank you," she said.

"No, thank you to talking about the job again, or to the job itself, or to—?"

"No, thank you to talking about the job anymore tonight."

He grinned. That grin that could turn her into mush, but now just turned her on.

She was an arm's length away from Dane but close enough to reach for his shirt buttons and unfasten just the one beneath the collar button that was already open.

Dane watched her do it, smiled again, but raised his eyebrows at her. "I wouldn't be taking advantage of you when you've hit a low point, would I?" he asked, his voice deeper than normal.

Vonni shrugged. "I'll be off-limits when I find a husband and settle down...." she warned.

"Ooh...let's not talk about *that*." He flinched.

Vonni laughed. "You're never getting married and I shouldn't, either?"

He grinned again. "I sure as hell don't want to talk about you with any other guy *now*."

Vonni liked that it bothered him on any level; she smiled and unfastened another button of his shirt.

He watched that happen, too, his hands on either side of his hips grasping the counter and remaining there.

When that button was open he once more looked into her eyes and said, "I really need to know that you're not just in shock from what happened tonight. Because seriously, Vonni, last night—"

Last night she'd stopped things.

"I know," she said. "But I'm not in shock. Tonight my eyes are wide-open—about everything. And I'm thinking…why not let there be something liberating about that?"

His hands moved from the counter's edge to rest lightly on her hips. "Eyes wide-open…" he repeated as if that was very important.

"Eyes wide-open," she confirmed. "There's just tonight…." A warning of her own.

"I'll take it," he declared.

Then he tugged her closer and kissed her. A first kiss kind of kiss that almost made her laugh because it was as if he was testing her, wondering if she would panic and run after all.

Vonni raised her hands to the back of his head, sensuously slid her fingers into his hair and tempted him to think again.

And she did feel him smile before his lips parted and the kiss got real.

Very, very real….

It jumped almost instantly from first kiss to kissing the way they had been the night before—mouths open and tongues teasing and tantalizing and inviting things to go so much further.

Still bracing his hips against the counter, Dane put

a foot out on either side of hers and pulled her between his legs—not so near that they were touching, but close. Then he put his arms around her so his hands were clasped at the small of her back as kissing became more intense, more hungry.

Just tonight, Vonni thought, and a determination not to waste a minute of it made her drag her hands from his hair to his shirt buttons again. She finished unfastening them all and tugged his shirttails from his waistband, exposing his torso—his broad chest and washboard abs.

Ah, his chest....

It had felt terrific through his shirt, but bare was so much better! Warm, smooth skin over rock-hard muscle—and his back was just as wonderful when she sluiced her hands around to it.

His shirt was a mere nuisance by then, so she got rid of it. Once she had, she reveled in being able to run her palms over biceps and shoulders and pectorals and the grand expanse of shoulders that gracefully V'd to a narrow waist she could use as a beltway to taut, taut sides and then to a great, hard, flat belly....

And all the while he merely kissed her and let her have her way with him.

Until he stopped.

Kissing her mouth, anyway.

Instead, he kissed her neck. And where her neck curved into her shoulder. And the hollow of her throat. And down as far as the cowl neckline dipped.

Which was about the time that his hands rose to the dress's zipper at the back.

A flutter of anticipation and nervousness went through her, but she merely did what she could to facilitate the zipper's descent to her tailbone.

Dane rose up to kiss her again then, a lazy, luxurious,

sexy kiss that was more a mating dance performed with their mouths than it was a kiss.

He brought his flattened palms under the edges of her dress and pressed the heels of his hands upward, opening it more with every inch he climbed.

One strap fell from her shoulder and the cowl dipped to the right, leaving Vonni to feel cooler air on the top half of her breast where it swelled above the navy blue lace strapless bra she was wearing.

And if her breasts didn't get more attention soon she thought she might scream!

But rather than getting what she wanted just yet, Dane paused in the kissing and merely rested his hands on her shoulder blades.

"Still sure?" he asked in a voice craggy with desire.

She tugged his bottom lip between her teeth and reached for the front of his waistband. "Positive," she whispered before she unhooked the button. His need for her alone helped lower the zipper.

It also helped unleash something wild and reckless and abandoned in them both when Dane recaptured her mouth with his and brought both hands to her breasts.

Vonni had wondered if he was holding in check all that she was, and now she got her answer as urgency erupted between them and swept them away.

His mouth was on hers as his hands worked at her breasts and released them from their lacy cups. Kneading and caressing and massaging, her nipples hardened to glass in palms where they fit to perfection.

Then he unhooked her bra and let it fall to the floor as he kissed the same path he'd followed before and took first one breast, then the other into his mouth.

His magic, magic mouth—it was warm, wet heaven sucking her in. His tongue traced the outer circle of her nipple, flicking at the crest, nipping with gentle teeth. It was an opus that awakened things in Vonni that filled her and propelled her and brought her alive with wants and needs for more.

Her dress was around her waist by then and he eased it down to fall to her ankles, leaving her in thigh-high nylons and string panties. In the brightly lit kitchen.

And she didn't even care because all she was thinking about was what had shocked her to her senses the night before—she was thinking about having him naked.

Only tonight it didn't shock her, it only spurred her on.

Finessing her hands to cup his rear end, she made enough room between him and the counter's edge to lower everything he had on from his waist down.

He laughed and growled a little at once, then hooked fingers in the strings of her bikini briefs and down those went, too, before he grabbed her derriere in a firm grip, lifted her and spun around to leave her sitting on the countertop.

He was kissing her again—crazy kissing that was all openmouthed and thrusting tongue and wicked temptation. Crazy kissing that he paused only for a split second as he reached for his pants to take his wallet from his pocket and retrieve a condom.

For now, he put the condom on the counter beside Vonni while he returned to kissing her, to having his hands on her breasts, on her backside, on her inner thighs and then in the junction between them where he did something remarkable with his thumbs that shot her instantly into a climax that came as a complete surprise and ended in some miracle that only made her ready for more.

Ready and dying for more....

She hadn't even realized that her arms had gone around him and she was clasping his tight rear end, but now she took one hand away from there and brought it around front, finding him and exploring the full length and thickness and magnificence of the man.

And he wasn't the only one of them who could escalate things; Vonni did a little of that herself, feasting on the sight of that nakedness she'd been craving, of that handsome face caught in closed-eyed passion, of that body all chiseled and cut and taut and muscular and masculine.

When he could take no more of what she was doing to him he retrieved the condom, applying it as he kissed her, as he sucked a breast into the cavern of his mouth again, as he churned up so much in her all over again that she didn't think she would be able to breathe for much longer without him inside of her.

And then he was. Carefully but not too slowly, as if he couldn't bear it another minute either, pulling her forward, to him, positioning her just so until he was deeply within her.

Pulsing and flexing and drawing out and then back in again, he positioned his hands on her backside, guiding her, helping her keep pace, to meet and match him with her ankles locked around him.

She held on to his massive shoulders and gave herself over to him, at the mercy of what was building from the very core of her. Building and building and building until it exploded into a second peak that made the first a mere shadow, sending the most exquisite pleasure all through her, taking her away to somewhere she'd never been before, somewhere where she was lost to everything but that divine culmination.

That divine culmination that was still rippling through her when his own erupted in him, too, sending him plunging to the depths of her and freezing his entire body into a tall mast of power and vitality and strength that Vonni could only cling to as she came back to herself, weak and spent and collapsing with her forehead on the shelf of his shoulder....

He wrapped his arms around her and held her, burying his own face in the side of her neck, kissing her, his breath hot and heavy against her skin.

"We're in your kitchen...." she whispered when the fact struck her all over again and she was able to speak.

Dane laughed—a rough, raspy, passion-ragged sound.

Then without saying anything, he slipped out of her, scooped his arms under her to form a seat and carried her from the kitchen with her legs still wrapped around his waist.

He took her up narrow service stairs to the second floor, into an enormous master suite with a king-size bed covered in a downy brown quilt.

At the bedside he continued to hold her, using only one arm to brace her while he flung back the quilt and the silk sheets underneath it and then laid her gently on the mattress and joined her there.

"Better?" he asked as he snaked an arm underneath her to curl her into his side and envelop her in his embrace.

"I don't know...." she said with a slight, self-conscious laugh, uncertain of anything now that exactly what she'd wanted had happened.

"Better," he declared, answering his own question. "This way we can rest a little and then try the traditional route."

That made Vonni laugh more genuinely. "Is that right?" she said as if he were being presumptuous.

"You gave me one night," he reminded. "If you think I'm not taking the *whole* night, you're wrong."

"The whole night...." she repeated as if letting it sink in but also with a hint of joyful anticipation.

"And some of the morning—brunch isn't until eleven after all...."

Brunch.

When he would go off and be a Camden.

And she would go home and decide if she was going to be a Camden employee.

When everything would become what it truly was.

But until then, she had the rest of tonight.

And part of tomorrow morning.

And nothing could make her think beyond that and being right where she was at that moment....

Chapter Ten

"Let me do what you wouldn't let GiGi do—let me convince you to come to brunch."

It was eight o'clock Sunday morning after a night like Vonni had never had. She and Dane had made love until they'd both dropped into exhausted sleep, bodies entwined, at 4:00 a.m. They'd slept a few hours and made love again. Each time better than the time before. And for at least half an hour now she'd been lying at Dane's side, her head in the hollow of his shoulder, one of her thighs resting over his, the length of their bodies joined seamlessly together. Just talking, neither of them making any move to leave his bed.

"No, the brunch is for family," Vonni said, sounding so, so much different than she felt.

Little by little as the night had gone on, she'd found herself slipping into old patterns. It had been so incredible being with him—not only making love but before and after, the talking, the kissing, the teasing and love play, the tender moments, the serious moments, the funny moments, *every* moment—that she'd begun to want more and more nights just like it. A forever of nights like it. She'd wanted it so much that it had started to seem inconceivable that he wouldn't want it, too.

Until she'd recalled that he didn't want it. That he didn't want forever with any woman. That he was unwaveringly devoted to his no-marriage, no-kids policy.

And she'd mentally shaken some sense into herself.

She'd been putting on the blinders again and she'd recognized it. She'd been forgetting that there was a component other than what *she* wanted. Other than how she wished things could be. And she'd reminded herself that she didn't have the power to change that other component. That she never had the power to change it.

She'd reminded herself that the past years of dating and disappointments had left her with nothing of what she wanted and that—as unwaveringly devoted as Dane was to his own goal—she needed to be just as dedicated to what she'd set out to do, too. To restoring herself, to reenergizing, to actually taking a step forward with a house, a dog, so she could begin to have some of what she wanted, and *then* find a like-minded man who was interested in building a life with her.

She'd reminded herself that to do anything else, to fall back into her old pattern with Dane and read more into this night than she should, would set her up for the biggest disappointment she'd ever suffered.

So outwardly she was being light, glib, carefree.

Even if, inwardly, there was far more turmoil roiling.

"This is it, remember?" she said, looking at her hand on his chest. "The window of opportunity is closing."

"You're really going to make me a one-night stand?"

She would never let him know how different she would make it if she could. "That was the deal."

"But we made the deal. We could alter it. You could come to brunch and when it's over we could have the rest of today—I could go with you to the animal shelter again, help with that horse-size sack of dog chow you bring them. Then we could go to dinner and have tonight…." He held her a little tighter. "Maybe we could even have until the lawyer you hire hashes out your contract with us and you actually sign it—I can do more talking about why you should come to work for us…."

And possibly if they saw more of each other he'd come to realize how good they were together and he'd fall in love with her and he'd want to spend the rest of his life with her—it was thinking like that that had cost her years with Tanner and David and Mark, years with countless other men she'd dated for a month or two or three in hopes that it would lead to having what she wanted because it would lead to them wanting it, too.

But Dane's no-illusions policy was saving her from that.

Even if saved was hardly how she felt….

"No," she said without any strength in her voice.

"So this is it?" he asked, rubbing her back and sounding as if he couldn't conceive that.

"Is the job offer not still on the table?" she asked.

"Oh, sure, it is. Of course. That goes without saying."

"I suppose if I get that lawyer he'll do whatever negotiating needs to be done, but we might see each other during the course of that, right?"

"I guess…." Dane said, even more confused.

"So this isn't the last time we'll ever see each other," Vonni concluded. "But it is the last time—"

"We're together," he said, finally understanding

where she was going. "The last time we're together the way we have been for the past two weeks. The way we have been since last night. The way we are now...." He flexed the biceps across her back to hug her a little.

Vonni hoped that he interpreted her silence as confirmation or merely an opportunity she was giving him to let things sink in.

But really she had to maintain that silence because she was working so hard at keeping her own emotions under control as the reality of how things would be from here on hit her, too. As she suffered the agony of facing that she wouldn't have any more of what she'd had with him—no more dinners, no more walks, no more talking and laughing and teasing. No Sundays like last Sunday shopping and running errands and just being together. Definitely no more nights—or mornings—with him....

She took a deep breath, careful to do it slowly so he wouldn't know she was struggling.

Then she said, "When I'm ready to get back on the dating circuit again, it's still marriage and a family that I want. Exactly what you *don't* want. And if we see each other anymore—for anything that isn't job related—I'll start to get invested. I'll start having hopes for more. I'll start to think that because things are good between us—"

"Ooh...things are *great* between us...." he muttered, and sighed as if it had been so great he didn't quite believe it.

But Vonni ignored the impulse she'd followed too many times in the past to run with that, to point out just how great things were and how they could get even better and that it was something they could have permanently.

Instead, she went on with what she was saying.

"I'll start to think that because things are good between us you must want what I want for us. And then
when that isn't true—" the words—or maybe it was
tears—clogged her throat and she had to swallow hard
to go on "—I just won't do that again. I know where
you stand. I appreciate knowing that and I respect it. We
said last night was just last night and that's what it was."

His arms tightened around her even more than they
had before and she wasn't sure why. Was he hanging
on to her and what they had because he didn't want to
lose it any more than she did?

Or was it merely one final, parting embrace, a reluctant validation that she was right?

The old Vonni would have grasped on to the hope
that his arms were tighter around her because he didn't
want to lose her, and she would have clung to that idea.

The new Vonni waited.

And when he squeezed even tighter and then loos-
ened his grip, she knew.

She knew nothing was different for him. That they
might have had a fantastic two weeks, an absolutely
amazing night, but he was now what he'd been from the
start—a man who had no intention of getting married,
of having kids. And that the only way to be with him
would be to deny herself what she wanted. And then find
herself once again having wasted precious time when it
ended and her life still wasn't where she wanted it to be.

So no matter how tempting it was to have more time
with him like what she'd already had, to put off everything just to be with him, to hope that eventually
he wouldn't want to lose her and so might change his
mind, she would not—could not—do it.

She patted his chest. She kneaded her fingers into
it for a moment before she gathered every bit of will-

power she'd ever had and pushed up and away from him, rolling to the side of the bed, using the sheet as a toga.

"So no brunch. No nothing from here on," she announced, thinking that she deserved an award for the performance that made it sound matter-of-fact and nothing at all like what she was feeling.

Dane didn't say anything, but she knew his eyes were on her and when she cast him a forced smile over her shoulder she saw the dark frown, the confusion that was on his handsome face.

He probably didn't know what *to* say, she thought. He was too nice a guy to say, *Yeah, you're right, I don't want to marry you any more than I want to marry anyone else, so if that's what you're holding out for, better to part ways now.*

And because he was too nice a guy to say that, he wasn't saying anything. He didn't want to hurt her— she knew that.

But she could maintain her performance for only so long and she knew she had to get out of there. In a hurry.

With the sheet wrapped around her she headed for the bedroom door. "I'm just going to throw my dress back on and go. Don't get up."

"Vonni—"

She shook her head fiercely and held up the hand that wasn't clamped on to the sheet in a death grip to stop whatever it was he was about to say.

"Let's just leave it at what it was," she said in a voice that cracked and made her hate herself. "I'll probably come to work for you and we'll just go on as if nothing ever happened."

"Vonni…" he said as if she were deluded to think that was possible.

But she cut him off again. "Say that's how it will be

or I *won't* come to work for Camdens," she threatened at the door, not turning to face him, not looking at him even over her shoulder because she just couldn't. And because she didn't want him to see the pain she knew by then had to be etched into her expression.

It was Dane who was silent this time and even though it was only a moment it seemed like an eternity.

Then, quietly, reluctantly and sounding as if he were just saying the words because she was making him, he said, "Come to work for us and we'll go on as if nothing ever happened."

"I'll let you know—or the lawyer will," she answered as if the job offer was the only thing they'd been talking about.

Then, using every ounce of oomph she had, she went out that bedroom door. She went down the service stairs to the kitchen where she got dressed quicker than she ever had in her life. Then she nearly ran out of that condo's front door barefoot and only carrying her shoes.

All the while hoping that Dane stayed away, hoping as she leaped into her car the very second she had the door open that he hadn't gotten out of bed or gone to the window to look down at her—or if he had, that he couldn't see her clearly enough to witness the tears that finally flooded down her cheeks.

Because her heart was breaking and she had no idea how she could have gotten in this deep this fast.

Especially having known right from the start that—for so many reasons—she could never have anything at all with Dane Camden.

"Dane. Here you are in the den," Dane's grandmother said. "You helped make all of this happen and every time I turn around, you're nowhere to be seen."

"Carter needed a bathroom run and asked me to take him. I was just coming back from that."

Partially true. Dane's three-year-old nephew *had* asked to be taken to the bathroom. But that was a while ago, and after sending Carter back to the brunch, Dane had hidden out in the den.

"What is wrong with you today?" GiGi demanded.

"Nothing." The biggest lie he'd ever told.

"The wedding was beautiful and we have you to thank for that," GiGi went on. "And you said you think the Hunter girl is going to do the wedding departments for us, didn't you?"

"I think so. I gave her John Beckman's name, told her to use him to hash out a contract she can be sure protects her—"

"Beckman will do that for sure—he'll skewer us. But no matter what it takes, it isn't too much—H.J. and your grandfather could have gone to prison for buying those formulas when they knew they were stolen, and this is merely just compensation. So we can check off making amends for another one of these messy things in our background because you did a good job on that, too. You should be out there celebrating, taking bows for both of the things you accomplished, and being happy."

He was sooo far from happy....

"True," he agreed halfheartedly.

"But you don't *look* happy.... Are you sick?" his grandmother continued to pry.

Illness seemed like a better excuse, so Dane seized it. "Maybe I'm a little hungover," he said. "All those toasts last night, you know."

"Well, take something for it and come back. You're my other man of the hour today for doing all you did and I want you out there, by my side, getting credit where credit is due."

"I'll get an aspirin or something and be right behind you," Dane assured her.

He wasn't in the least hungover, so he had no need for medication but he figured that pretending he was going to take something would buy him at least a few more minutes to himself.

And he needed to be by himself. He was just a damn wreck today and in no mood for socializing.

But liquor wasn't to blame. He hadn't had much to drink at all last night.

What he'd had was a night to top all nights with Vonni.

Maybe he had a Vonni hangover.

Except that he'd had hangovers before and in the midst of them the last thing he even wanted to think about was whatever had given him the hangover in the first place.

But today Vonni was all he could think about.

And while a hangover left a bad taste and an inclination toward never indulging again, he certainly didn't feel that way about Vonni.

That was the problem.

He wanted to indulge again and she'd shut him down.

Without him seeing it coming.

When it came to women, he didn't look at things long-range. His no-marriage policy just didn't call for that. He tended to be in the moment with them, and he guessed that he'd been so in the moment with Vonni that she'd taken him by surprise. But damn if it hadn't hit him like a battering ram.

While he was lying in bed with her this morning, it had been unfathomable that *everything* was about to come crashing to a conclusion despite the ground rules they'd agreed on for that exact thing. It had been unfathomable to think that last night was the one and only night he was going to get with her, that all that had gone on between them for the past two weeks was over and never to be repeated. Facing that had flattened him.

He'd just lain there in bed, baffled by the fact that what was happening was happening, unable to stop it.

Because how could he stop it when everything Vonni had said was the truth?

He'd been as clear with her as he was with every woman—he didn't want marriage, he didn't want to do the whole family thing.

And she'd been clear with him—she *did* want marriage, she did want the whole family thing. So much that she'd approached it like a second job and intended to go back to that after this temporary breather she was taking.

Given how clear they'd both been about what they wanted and didn't want, what could he have possibly said to argue with her exit?

Nothing—that was the answer. There wasn't a single damn thing he could have said.

But why had it been so gut-wrenching? he kept asking himself as he stood at one of the windows in the den and looked out at the cars parked in the drive. Why was his gut *still* wrenched? Why was he twisted into knots and feeling worse than any hangover had ever left him?

He just kept trying to figure that out....

When he and Nessa had parted ways for her to go to medical school, when Donna had gone overseas to take pictures, he hadn't felt like this. He had not been twisted in knots. He'd said goodbye to them, wished them well and told them to keep in touch.

When Rebecca had decided she did want marriage

and a family after all, it had been unpleasant having her try to convince him to marry her. But he had not been twisted in knots even though he had cared that things between them had reached that impasse and so would stop.

But hell, even in the middle of Rebecca arguing her case it had occurred to him that she was perfect for Buzzy and that Buzzy would be interested.

Now just the thought of Vonni ultimately finding some guy who would want what she wanted made him recoil. It made him feel almost as sick as if he did have a hangover.

And equally as strange was how he'd felt since arriving at GiGi's house for brunch today.

He'd felt rotten since Vonni had left but it had gotten even worse here.

Not ever before had it bothered him to be on his own at these family things. If he was involved with someone, he included her in family events and occasions, but if he wasn't, coming solo had been just fine. Not once had he looked at siblings or cousins who were coupled up with someone and felt envious. Felt alone and…

Alone and what?

He analyzed his emotions, trying to put a name to them, and then realized that he was miserable—that was how he'd felt in spades since getting to GiGi's house—alone and miserable. And as if something was missing for him.

Never before had he felt that way.

But today…

Today was god-awful.

God-awful and grim.

It was like being in some kind of nightmare where he noticed every single glance that passed between those couples. Every secret smile. Every private joke being shared. Every touch. Every shoulder nudge. *Everything!*

And each and every single damn one of those things had stabbed at him and made him think of Vonni. Made him want her and wish she was there with him so he could be having those same things with her.

It was so damn bad that he couldn't stand being in that group and having it happen again and again.

So he kept escaping into the house, away from the brunch on the patio....

He closed his eyes and suffered the ripple of just how rotten he felt even thinking about what was going on out there—with Lang and Heddy, Jani and Gideon, Seth and Lacey, Cade and Nati, GiGi and Jonah....

He'd never experienced anything like it before, and he didn't know what to do with himself.

He didn't know how to make himself feel better. How to get out of this black hole when Vonni was the only thing he could think of that made him see light.

And there was just one way to have Vonni....

He dropped his head back and looked up at the summer sky outside the window in disbelief.

Having Vonni required him to do exactly what he'd sworn he would never do. What he hadn't wanted to do.

But suddenly he wasn't so sure he didn't want to do it....

Not when he was thinking about doing it with Vonni.

Did that mean that he *did* want to get married now? he wondered, shocked at himself. That he *did* want to have kids and do the whole domestic dance?

You better really think about this....

Coupling up with Vonni...

Marriage.

Kids.

Living with another person.

Being answerable to that other person. Not coming and going as he pleased. Adapting to someone else's schedules and needs and tastes.

And kids? The constant caretaking and doing for and looking out for. The homework. The school functions and soccer games and birthday parties. All that he'd done until he was blue in the face being one of the oldest of ten kids in the same household....

And yet...

Why was it that when he pictured doing all of that again—every bit of it—with Vonni, it wasn't *un*appealing?

Now, *that* was odd.

But he started to think about last night, about this morning, about how it had felt to have Vonni in his house, in his bed. And it occurred to him that that had been different than with any other woman, too.

Regardless of how long he was with a woman, of how much he cared for her, he'd refused to cohabitate. As far as he was concerned, living together was just marriage without the paperwork and it wasn't the paperwork he objected to.

And when a woman he was involved with spent the night he always felt as if he had a houseguest—someone who, regardless of how much he liked them and liked being with them—didn't quite fit. It somehow put things out of balance and made him less comfortable than when he was on his own.

But now that he thought about it, he realized that that wasn't how it had been last night. Last night had been great. It had been just the way every other minute with Vonni had been since he'd met her—easy, comfortable, relaxed....

Better even...

Better?

Not only had it seemed as if she fit, but he'd felt *better* having her there?

Come on, he silently cajoled himself in disbelief.

But it was true.

And no matter how much he picked at it and analyzed it and tried to deny it, the truth was that, yes, being with Vonni, having Vonni in his house, in his bed, had actually felt *better* than being alone....

Just the way having her here today would have made him feel better.

"So I'm a hypocrite," he said to himself.

But he wasn't, and as the conclusions he'd come to sank in, he understood why.

He hadn't been posturing or putting on a false front when he'd said he didn't want to ever get married or have a family or do the domestic thing again. He'd meant it wholeheartedly.

He just hadn't known that it wouldn't stay true if he met that Certain Someone.

That just one Certain Someone could turn his whole world upside down. Fast. And be a complete and total game changer.

For him, that one Certain Someone was Vonni.

"ZsiZsi says what're you still doin' in here and come out!"

It was Lang's son Carter's voice—and difficulty saying *G's*—that barged into Dane's thoughts.

He turned to face the little boy, and just seeing him made Dane smile.

He loved Carter and had a lot of fun with him—Fun Uncle Dane.

And as Fun Uncle Dane, he'd taken Carter to the zoo, to the park, swimming. He did whatever needed to be done with him if he was in the best position to do it—like taking him to the bathroom a little while ago.

None of it had been such a big deal. And now, thinking of having kids of his own—kids who were his and Vonni's—with Vonni right there beside him, it just didn't seem the way it always had to him. It didn't seem like the chore it had been when he was a kid himself, looking after younger siblings and cousins. It seemed okay. And he was somehow all for it.

"I'll be right there, buddy," he told Carter.

"ZsiZsi says to drag you," Carter announced, charging him, grabbing him around the leg as if it was a tree trunk and trying to drag him.

Dane laughed at the attempt and took a step with the leg Carter clung to. "I'll drag you," he told the three-year-old who was giggling at the ride.

But Dane did finally leave the den—with Carter attached to his leg—and headed back to the brunch, hoping still that it wouldn't last much longer.

Only now he wasn't hoping that so he could escape the rotten feelings the gathering had been giving him.

Now he hoped it wouldn't last much longer because he had somewhere else he needed to go before he could get to Vonni.

And getting to Vonni as soon as he could was suddenly the most important thing he'd ever done....

Chapter Eleven

"Hi, Mom." It was early Sunday evening when Vonni connected with Elizabeth for their video chat on the computer.

Because she hadn't wanted to talk to her mother—or let her mother see her—so soon after leaving Dane's house this morning, Vonni had emailed, said she had a lot to do and asked to postpone their usual Sunday-morning date until six o'clock tonight.

It was actually six-thirty and Vonni didn't feel any better than she had when she'd left Dane. But she had the crying under control and after spending her Sunday afternoon at the animal shelter with Charlie she'd applied cold compresses to her eyes, then done her makeup to hide the telltale signs of more tears on the way home from the shelter.

She'd also done her hair so it was loose around her shoulders. She'd been afraid that pulling it back might draw undue attention to how her eyes were red under the concealer she'd used.

"Hi, honey," Elizabeth responded from in front of her own computer. "Did you get everything done that you needed to today?"

"Pretty much," Vonni answered. "How was your day?"

"Audie and I took Dashell to the airport—he left today—and that was about all we did," Elizabeth said cheerily. "If I'd have talked to you this morning I was going to ask you to pick Dashell up in Denver so you could meet him. But when I got your email I thought you probably wouldn't have the time...."

"I wouldn't have," Vonni said, too emotionally worn out to repeat the fact that she had no interest in being hooked up with her mother's boyfriend's single son.

Then Elizabeth leaned closer to the screen and said, "Have you been crying? You always get those red cheeks when you've been crying...."

"Maybe I just got a little too much sun today with Charlie," Vonni said, thinking it was a plausible excuse. There was no way she was telling her mother about Dane and their night together. Or how incredibly— and surprisingly—rocked she'd been by getting up this morning to the realization that she had to put a stop to everything with Dane. Or how she'd felt all day long as if an important, long-term, serious relationship had just ended—which didn't make any sense at all.

So to avoid getting into it, she said, "I did get some kind of upsetting news, though...."

She went on to tell her mother about the Burkes, the refusal to give her a partnership again and the edict from Howard Burke that she teach his new fiancée how to do her job. "At which point it looks like Mr. Burke 'could give her the shop as a wedding gift and—if I stayed—I'd just be working for her...."

It was somewhat comforting to Vonni to listen to her mother's outrage on her behalf. When Elizabeth had vented for a while she settled down some and said, "What are you going to do?"

"Well..." Vonni shrugged. "I'm going to finish out the weddings that are coming up for the next four weeks—I don't want to abandon my brides at the last minute and four weeks seems like a reasonable amount of time—"

"What about the ones after that? You've still done the work and those brides are expecting you to coordinate, too."

"I know," Vonni said, feeling guilty about that. "But there's no time I can leave when that won't be true—I've put in two and three months of work and gotten to know the brides from weddings that won't happen until Christmas. One that's a New Year's Eve wedding. I'll just have to use the next four weeks to introduce Mr. Burke's fiancée to everyone and hope that they like her and that I can have her up to speed by the time their big day arrives and she's their coordinator. None of us really have a choice...."

Vonni paused before she shored up her courage and said, "Then I think I'm going to take the job with Camdens."

There wasn't a lot of conviction in her words because as the day had worn on she'd worried more and more about it.

Not about the job itself, but about seeing Dane again.

Even if it was only here and there during the negotiations and contract signing, even if there was only a small chance of running into him when she *was* working within the Camden organization, she still wasn't too sure she could handle it. So if she felt as if she had another, better option, she probably *wouldn't* accept the Camden offer. But it was still an offer too good to refuse, especially now that she was facing what she was facing at Burke's Weddings.

She just hoped that today was a particularly bad day. That she would come out of this funk, stop thinking about Dane, stop wanting Dane, stop wishing things could be different between them, so that a glimpse of him every now and then would come to mean nothing.

After all, she'd reasoned with herself, between having the rug pulled out from under her at Burke's Weddings and then having to come up for air after last night with Dane only to end things with him, she was feeling unusually raw. But maybe in a few days, when the shock had worn off, when she'd put in her notice with the Burkes and gotten a lawyer to handle Camdens, she would feel better and everything would be okay.

"What do you think about me taking the Camdens offer?" she asked her mother.

"I'd want you to do it cautiously...." Elizabeth said.

"I have the name of a lawyer Dane Camden says hates the Camdens. Dane says the lawyer will make sure the deal is all to my benefit if I hire him to negotiate a contract. I haven't talked to the lawyer yet—I'll call him tomorrow and see what he has to say—but between the two of us and whatever you can think of, too, I'll try to have all my bases covered. Dane says I can even add a clause that gives me enough out-the-door money—if for any reason I end up leaving—to start my own business."

"So they really are trying to make up for what they did to Grampa."

"He didn't say that outright, but yes, I think that's what's behind this."

"Not that you aren't fantastic at what you do, honey. Or that getting you wouldn't be *huge* for them."

Vonni smiled weakly at her mother's praise. "Absolutely," she said facetiously, even though she didn't doubt her own job skills. "But what do you think about that—going to work for the people who did what they did to Grampa?"

"I can tell you what your grandfather would say if he was here—he'd say this is good coming from bad, and he'd be all for it."

"You think so?"

"He would want to know you're protected—you know he kicked himself for not being smarter about keeping his formulas from *anyone* being able to get their hands on them. But I'm glad to hear you'll get a lawyer to look out for your best interests—and all the better if it's someone who doesn't like the Camdens. Maybe he'll be especially tough on them and make sure you come out ahead no matter what."

"But you don't think Grampa would feel like I've crossed over to an enemy camp?"

"Honey, really, I think it would give him some satisfaction to know that the Camdens are willing to do anything to have you and that you'll make them pay dearly for it—he'd see that as a win for him in the end. He'd say it's just what the Camdens deserve—having to put a whole lot of money in the Hunters' pockets after all, only this time it's on the up-and-up and going into the right pocket."

That did sound like what Vonni remembered of her grandfather.

"So just stick it to them—for Grampa's sake and for your own," her mother concluded.

Vonni laughed. "I'll do my best."

"Now tell me about the house—you emailed that you found one after we talked last Sunday?"

Vonni told her mother all about that and was in the process of giving her the website address where her mother could see pictures of the place when there was a knock on her apartment door.

"That's probably Mrs. Dunwilly," Vonni said.

She'd run into Mrs. Dunwilly when she'd come up the outside stairs in tears this morning. Seeing that had alarmed the elderly woman, who had stopped to ask what was wrong. Vonni had only claimed to have job problems, expressed her appreciation for Mrs. Dunwilly's concern and said she'd be fine.

But obviously wanting to comfort her, Mrs. Dunwilly had vowed to check on her later to see if she was all right and bring her a loaf of the homemade banana bread she was making this afternoon.

Vonni opted to leave out the emotional part of that encounter and told her mother only about the banana bread.

"Well, go and have your company," Vonni's mother said. "Audie and I are headed out for dinner, anyway. But why don't we do this again Tuesday or Wednesday night so you can tell me about the house inspection and letting the Burkes know you're quitting and what the lawyer says and...you just have too much going on to wait a week, honey."

"Okay," Vonni agreed before they said a quick goodbye and Vonni disconnected just as the second knock sounded.

"Coming," she called, hoping that her neighbor—

who, despite never letting any small infraction go unnoticed or unreported, also had a caring side—wouldn't stay long.

She just wasn't up to any more talking. Or thinking. Or even being awake. She felt so awful she thought that as soon as she could get Mrs. Dunwilly to leave she was going to crawl into her bed, pull the covers over her head and just pray for a miracle to wipe away all memory of Dane Camden so she could feel better tomorrow.

And it would take a miracle for her to feel better tomorrow, she thought as she took a deep breath and tried to seem okay as she opened the door.

Not to Mrs. Dunwilly at all....

"Dane."

Her shock at seeing him was compounded by the fact that not only was he there, he was carrying a dog in each arm—her dog, Charlie, and the other dog named Ralph that they'd played with at the shelter last Sunday and that Vonni had seen again today when she'd been there earlier.

Ralph stayed put. But Charlie recognized Vonni, got excited and tried to leap out of Dane's grasp to get to her.

Vonni caught him as Dane said a simple, "Hi."

"Hi..." she echoed, her own voice laden with questions as she settled Charlie against her, wondering what in the world was going on. She was completely at the mercy of emotions warring between the thrill of seeing Dane and wishing he wasn't there.

Because she knew herself. And she knew that she just needed to sever things or she wasn't going to be able to resist him. That was why she'd left this morning; that was why she'd told him they couldn't be together anymore.

And now here he was.

When she stood frozen and unsure what to do, Dane said, "Better let me in before Mrs. Dunwilly sees the dogs." He nodded over his shoulder at her neighbor's door.

"That's who I thought you were," Vonni said, still hesitating because she was aware of how risky it was to let him into her apartment.

She was wearing summer-weight green-and-white polka-dot pajama pants and a bright green T-shirt that was loose enough to conceal the fact that she was bra-less. The loungewear just didn't feel like enough armor against the draw of Dane.

And he was dressed in jeans and a plain black polo shirt that made him look so good it flashed through her mind that she needed him the way she needed air to breathe.

But she couldn't have him, so certainly letting him in was dangerous. The problem was, when she'd left him this morning, she'd concealed her true feelings for him, playing it light and breezy, and she couldn't suddenly let those true feelings show and make a drama out of him being there. No matter how dramatic it felt to her.

So she stepped back into the apartment with Charlie and let Dane and Ralph in, closing the door behind them.

"You can put him down," she said with a nod at Ralph as she set Charlie on the floor and went to the kitchen to get the dogs a bowl of water and some treats.

"What's going on?" she asked then, trying to sound matter-of-fact. Trying to conceal that she'd just had the worst day she could ever remember having, and was now desperately worried that he was going to suggest what David had suggested when she'd broken up with him—that while she was looking for a husband the two of them could become friends with benefits. Turning down that idea with David had been easy. She wasn't sure she could turn anything down with Dane....

"What's going on," he parroted, sitting on the arm of her sofa, "is something big."

"Did the shelter burn down after I left?" she asked because the first thing she couldn't figure out was why the dogs were with him.

He laughed even as his brow beetled in confusion of his own. "No, the shelter didn't burn down."

"I just don't understand why you're here, let alone how you got Charlie and Ralph...."

Dane's perplexity disappeared and only a smile remained. "I know you aren't a big sports enthusiast but even so, you must know how sometimes—let's say in a big football game—one team can be winning because the other team isn't doing anything right, and the end just seems like a given. And then something happens— an unbelievable pass or intercept or something—and all of a sudden everything turns around. Completely around—"

"Sure, I've heard of that." Which still didn't explain the dogs...

"Well, that happened to me today," Dane said.

Concern for him overruled her own anxieties. "Were you in an accident or something? Is your family okay— the wedding wasn't too much for your grandmother or her groom, was it?"

He laughed again. "Wow, you're really going to the dark side, aren't you? The animal shelter burning down, me being in an accident, GiGi or Jonah dropping from too much wedding excitement...."

Dark and dismal—that was how she'd felt all day, so

Vonni thought that it followed that she'd be expecting the worst of this visit. But she couldn't say that so she said, "I'm just trying to understand…."

"What happened to me today was that you left this morning."

"And that was an unbelievable pass or an intercept or something?"

"It was. Because it turned things around for me and made me realize that *you* are the game changer for me."

Vonni had kept her distance, remaining standing just outside of her kitchen. But she wasn't sure she was hearing correctly, and there were still too many warring emotions inside of her making her dizzy. She thought she'd better sit down. So she went to the easy chair across from the sofa.

"Before you, Vonni," Dane went on, "I thought I knew what I wanted. I thought I had it all figured out, all under control. I honestly didn't want any more of family life. And to tell you the truth, every Sunday dinner at GiGi's brought it home to me—I'd be there with everybody, doing the family thing all over again—enjoying it—but still, when it was over, I liked getting back to my nice quiet house, doing whatever I pleased, answering to no one but myself. It seemed like the perfect balance—all the family and company I wanted when I was with everybody else, peace and quiet when I left. But today…" He shook his head.

"Today something happened that's never happened before. It was like some piece of me was missing without you there. I might as well have gone without pants on or something. And that got me to thinking about how other things aren't the same with you, either—"

He talked about not feeling the way he had in the past about having someone else in his house, in his bed, and how that had led him to think about doing so many other things with her.

"Here's the dumbest-sounding thing I'm ever going to say to you," he said then. "All the things I thought I never wanted to do again, I just didn't want to do without you. Even though I didn't know you. Because now that I do know you, it changes the game. It changes everything."

He got up from the arm of the chair and crossed to her, hunkering down on his heels in front of her and taking her hands in his. "When I do things with you, when I think of having things with you—like kids— it's like nothing I ever felt before. And the reason is— and this seems pretty strange to say at my age—while I've cared about other women and even been in deep with a few of them, I've never *loved* anyone else. But I do love you."

He called Charlie over to them and Ralph came along.

"Sorry, Big R, but this time I only need your buddy," he told the scruffy black-and-brown mutt as he picked up the schnauzer.

"Big R?" Vonni said.

"He thinks he's *huge,*" Dane said with a laugh before he set Charlie in her lap and confused her yet again.

Then he pointed out something she hadn't noticed before. A gold ring set with garnets that Charlie's collar was hooked through.

"So this is what I did," he said then. "I weighed what was more likely to convince you—diamonds or dogs— and I decided to go with dogs. So the ring is only a space holder that I borrowed from my grandmother until I can get one of your own, and I went to the shelter and told them I needed dogs—Charlie for you and Ralph for me so you'll see that I *am* willing to make commitments to you in every way you want."

"And they just let you take my dog?"

"They made me leave my driver's license in case I was lying and trying to steal old One-Eyed Charlie out from under you, but here I am with these two to let you know that whatever you want, I want, too. That I'm all-in, Vonni. And that if you and Charlie will have me and Ralph, I'd like it if you'd marry me...."

"You're the guy who was never—*ever*—getting married," Vonni said dimly because too much had come at her at once and her head was spinning.

"I *was* that guy. I'm not anymore—"

"In just one day?" Vonni said, her skepticism sounding in her voice.

"It didn't even take that long for me to realize that now I'm just a guy who met the one person he wants to be with for the rest of his life and is willing to do whatever it takes to get that."

"Dogs, marriage, kids—those are lifetime commitments, Dane," she said quietly. "They aren't just... concessions you make. I want those things, but I want them with someone who wants them, too. For real, not just because he feels forced into it or even because there's some novelty to it for the moment. I won't always be *new* to you, and going to school programs and soccer games with me will eventually just be going to school programs and soccer games. If you've had your fill of family life, won't you reach that saturation point again and just want out?"

"No, I won't. Because I thought family life would be family life no matter what, and that I was done with it. What I didn't know was that when you find that one person you want to actually have a life with, a family of your own with, it all feels different. It all feels as if it's the first time it's ever happened to anyone. The thought of marrying and compromising and living with someone who isn't you still *doesn't* appeal to me. But I can't stand the thought of going back to my own house tonight without you. The thought of having kids, if you aren't their mother, isn't what I want. But I *do* want kids with *you*—"

Vonni shook her head slowly, still doubting this. Still doubting him.

But Dane didn't waver. He took the ring off Charlie's collar, let Charlie jump down from Vonni's lap and rested his elbows on her knees.

"You want a house and a dog and marriage and kids," he said then. "You've always known that and have been looking for someone who will want it, too. I didn't want that stuff until I met you. Now I only want it *with* you. We didn't come to it from the same angle, Vonni, but we both came to it—"

Then something else seemed to strike him and he veered back a little and sobered a lot.

"Unless… Wow. Am I doing what you said you've done before? Am I just figuring that because I want you, you must want me, too? And you don't…."

That made Vonni laugh. Wryly, but laugh just the same. And for some reason she didn't understand it also made her eyes fill with tears again today.

"I do want you. But—"

"Should I have gone with the diamonds and not the dogs?" he half joked.

"I'm just afraid that when the bloom wears off—"

"It isn't a bloom, Vonni. I *love* you. Deep down. With all my heart. Believe me when I tell you that it isn't some passing thing that will wear off. It's not an infatuation. I know when I've found the one person on this planet who I was meant to be with, who I was meant to do these things with. I want you to be my wife. I want to go through the rest of my life with you by my side. I want you to know that you're right—it *is* possible for two people to find each other, make a life together, build on it and live happily ever after because that's what we do to prove it."

Vonni had to think about all of that.

She was not only suddenly being offered everything she'd ever wanted, but by a man she wanted more than any man she'd ever known.

It seemed too good to be true, and that terrified her.

In the past she'd let herself believe that the man she was with would come around to wanting marriage and family. She'd banked on him changing his mind.

And now that one was right here in front of her, swearing to her that he had, she didn't know if she could trust it....

She'd already learned well that she didn't have the power to change a man's mind. That regardless of what she wanted or what she did or how long she waited, she couldn't make it happen.

But she'd left Dane this morning. She hadn't tried to convince him of anything. She hadn't tried to prove anything or open his eyes to anything.

And he'd come to all these conclusions himself. This was *his* idea. *His* plan. *His* proposal.

Complete with dogs....

She'd refused to let herself hope for more from him this morning. But had she turned so jaded that she couldn't believe that he could come to see how good they were together, all that they could have together, on his own?

Or was she fooling herself again by allowing herself to believe things she shouldn't just because she wanted to?

She raised a hand to his cheek, laying the backs of her fingers to it. Trying so hard to know...

And as she looked at that handsome face, into the oh-so-blue eyes of this man whom she suddenly admitted to herself she loved beyond anything she'd ever thought possible, it occurred to her that this was Dane. That what had developed between them had come naturally, without pretense or plan or plot or smokescreens on either of their parts. She'd been herself with him. And he'd been himself.

And out of that had come this connection without any attempt to make a connection.

It struck her then that maybe that made what they had more real at its root.

And that maybe, without any subterfuge to muddle it, that was why it had been able to grow and blossom so quickly.

Why she could trust it.

And trust this straightforward man she didn't feel complete without.

This person who listened to her and cared what she thought. This person who looked out for her and made her feel valued and respected and appreciated.

This person who—when her eyes met his in a crowded room—made her feel like she was the most important, most special woman there.

And little by little she began to think that maybe—finally—she really had found someone who felt about her what she felt about him.

Someone who could recognize what they could have together the way she did.

Someone who could want what she wanted when he saw it through her.

Even if it meant a very big change for him....

"You're sure...." she heard herself whisper.

"I'm so sure that I'm going to tell you to have that lawyer who hates all Camdens hammer out a prenuptial agreement when he hammers out the business contract, too—"

"The marriage proposal doesn't cancel out the job offer?"

He laughed. "It's a family business, and I may not mix business and pleasure, but making you family is the way around that. And I'm so sure I want you to be my family that I'm not leaving here tonight without you—and not just because Mrs. Dunwilly won't let you keep the dogs here. It's because I just plain can't leave here without you. I'm so sure that I'm going to call your Realtor tomorrow and have him put my condo on the market because I know that when you called my place *fancy* you were being nice to avoid saying that you hate it—"

Vonni laughed at the fact that he knew her so well that he'd seen through that, too. It also made the tears fall.

Tears he brushed away with gentle hands.

"I'm so sure," he went on, "that I'm going to cover any money lost by pulling out of that offer you made on that little cracker box of a house because we'll need a much bigger one. I'm so sure," he said, his voice getting very quiet and deep, "that you can tell me how and when and where you want to get married and no matter what, I'll make it happen. Because I'm sure that I love you, Vonni, and that I don't want to go another hour without you."

"I love you, too," Vonni finally confessed, turning her hand over to cup her palm to his chiseled cheek.

"Does that mean that you'll marry me?"

"It does," she said.

The ring he slipped on her finger then was a cocktail ring but it didn't matter to Vonni. Nothing mattered to her as Dane got to his feet, pulled her to hers and kissed her then, cradling her face between both of his big hands, cherishing her.

And as Vonni gave herself over to that kiss, to that man, to the future she'd just agreed to have with him, she silently apologized to the spirit of her grandfather, hoping he would feel that the wrong done to him years ago could just be water under the bridge.

The bridge that had brought her Dane.

And the fulfillment—finally—of everything she'd always wanted.

* * * * *

Be sure not to miss other books in
USA TODAY *bestselling author*
Victoria Pade's series,
THE CAMDENS OF COLORADO:

CORNER-OFFICE COURTSHIP
A BABY IN THE BARGAIN
IT'S A BOY!

Available from Harlequin Special Edition!

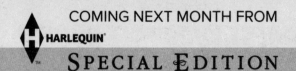

COMING NEXT MONTH FROM

HARLEQUIN

SPECIAL EDITION

Available April 15, 2014

#2329 THE PRINCE'S CINDERELLA BRIDE
The Bravo Royales • by Christine Rimmer
Lani Vasquez cherishes her role as nanny to the Montedoran royal children—particularly since it offers proximity to her good friend, the handsome Prince Maximilian. Max has grieved his lost wife for years, but this Prince Charming is ready for the next chapter of his love story—and his Cinderella is right under his nose.

#2330 FALLING FOR FORTUNE
The Fortunes of Texas: Welcome to Horseback Hollow
by Nancy Robards Thompson
Christopher Fortune has gladly embraced the wealth and power of his newfound family name. But not everyone's as impressed by the Fortune legacy. His new coworker, Kinsley Aaron, worked for everything she ever got, and Chris's newly entitled attitude rubs her the wrong way. Now Chris will have to earn Kinsley's love—and his Fortune fairy-tale ending....

#2331 THE HUSBAND LIST
Rx for Love • by Cindy Kirk
Great job? Check. Hunky hubby? Not so much. Dr. Mitzi Sanchez has her life just where she wants it—except for the husband she's always dreamed of. She creates a checklist for her perfect man—but she insists pilot Keenan McGregor isn't it. With a bit of luck, Keenan might blow Mitzi's expectations sky-high....

#2332 HEALED WITH A KISS
Bride Mountain • by Gina Wilkins
Both burned by love, wedding planner Alexis Mosley and innkeeper Logan Carmichael aren't looking for anything serious when they plunge into a passionate affair. Little by little, though, what starts as a no-strings-attached fling evolves into something much deeper. Can they heal their emotional wounds to start afresh, or will the ghosts of relationships past haunt them forever?

#2333 GROOMED FOR LOVE
Sweet Springs, Texas • by Helen R. Myers
Due to her declining sight, Rylie Quinn abandoned her dreams of becoming a veterinarian and moved to Sweet Springs, Texas, as an animal groomer. She just wants to get on with her life—something that irritating attorney Noah Prescott won't allow her to do. He's determined to dig up Rylie's past, and, as he and Rylie butt heads, true love might just rear its own.

#2334 THE BACHELOR DOCTOR'S BRIDE
The Doctors MacDowell • by Caro Carson
Bright, free-spirited and bubbly, Diana Connor gets under detached cardiologist Quinn MacDowell's skin...and not in a way he'd care to admit. When the two are forced to work together at a field clinic, Quinn begins to see just how caring Diana is and how well she interacts with patients. This heart doctor might just need a bit of Diana's medicine for himself....

YOU CAN FIND MORE INFORMATION ON UPCOMING HARLEQUIN® TITLES, FREE EXCERPTS AND MORE AT WWW.HARLEQUIN.COM.

HSECNM0414

REQUEST YOUR FREE BOOKS!
2 FREE NOVELS PLUS 2 FREE GIFTS!

HARLEQUIN®

SPECIAL EDITION

Life, Love & Family

YES! Please send me 2 FREE Harlequin® Special Edition novels and my 2 FREE gifts (gifts are worth about $10). After receiving them, if I don't wish to receive any more books, I can return the shipping statement marked "cancel." If I don't cancel, I will receive 6 brand-new novels every month and be billed just $4.74 per book in the U.S. or $5.24 per book in Canada. That's a savings of at least 14% off the cover price! It's quite a bargain! Shipping and handling is just 50¢ per book in the U.S. and 75¢ per book in Canada.* I understand that accepting the 2 free books and gifts places me under no obligation to buy anything. I can always return a shipment and cancel at any time. Even if I never buy another book, the two free books and gifts are mine to keep forever.

235/335 HDN F45Y

Name	(PLEASE PRINT)	
Address		Apt. #
City	State/Prov.	Zip/Postal Code

Signature (if under 18, a parent or guardian must sign)

Mail to the **Harlequin® Reader Service:**
IN U.S.A.: P.O. Box 1867, Buffalo, NY 14240-1867
IN CANADA: P.O. Box 609, Fort Erie, Ontario L2A 5X3

Want to try two free books from another line?
Call 1-800-873-8635 or visit www.ReaderService.com.

* Terms and prices subject to change without notice. Prices do not include applicable taxes. Sales tax applicable in N.Y. Canadian residents will be charged applicable taxes. Offer not valid in Quebec. This offer is limited to one order per household. Not valid for current subscribers to Harlequin Special Edition books. All orders subject to credit approval. Credit or debit balances in a customer's account(s) may be offset by any other outstanding balance owed by or to the customer. Please allow 4 to 6 weeks for delivery. Offer available while quantities last.

Your Privacy—The Harlequin® Reader Service is committed to protecting your privacy. Our Privacy Policy is available online at www.ReaderService.com or upon request from the Harlequin Reader Service.

We make a portion of our mailing list available to reputable third parties that offer products we believe may interest you. If you prefer that we not exchange your name with third parties, or if you wish to clarify or modify your communication preferences, please visit us at www.ReaderService.com/consumerschoice or write to us at Harlequin Reader Service Preference Service, P.O. Box 9062, Buffalo, NY 14269. Include your complete name and address.

HSE13R

***

He was fresh out of new tactics and had no clue how to get her to let down her guard. Plus he had a very strong feeling that he'd pushed her as far as she would go for now. This was looking to be an extended campaign. He didn't like that, but if it was the only way to finally reach her, so be it. "I'll be seeing you in the library—where you will no longer scuttle away every time I get near you."

A hint of the old humor flashed in her eyes. "I never scuttle."

"Scamper? Dart? Dash?"

"Stop it." Her mouth twitched. A good sign, he told himself.

"Promise me you won't run off the next time we meet."

The spark of humor winked out. "I just don't like this."

"You've already said that. I'm going to show you there's nothing to be afraid of. Do we have an understanding?"

"Oh, Max..."

"Say yes."

And finally, she gave in and said the words he needed to hear. "Yes. I'll, um, look forward to seeing you."

He didn't believe her. How could he believe her when she sounded so grim, when that mouth he wanted beneath his own was twisted with resignation? He didn't believe her, and he almost wished he could give her what she said she wanted, let her go, say goodbye. He almost wished he could *not* care.

But he'd had so many years of not caring. Years and years when he'd told himself that not caring was for the best.

And then the small, dark-haired woman in front of him changed everything.

***

Enjoy this sneak peek from Christine Rimmer's
THE PRINCE'S CINDERELLA BRIDE,
the latest installment in her Harlequin® Special Edition
miniseries **THE BRAVO ROYALES,** *on sale May 2014!*

⬧ HARLEQUIN®

SPECIAL EDITION

Life, Love and Family

Coming in May 2014

HEALED WITH A KISS
by reader-favorite author
Gina Wilkins

Both burned by love, wedding planner Alexis Mosley and innkeeper Logan Carmichael aren't looking for anything serious when they plunge into a passionate affair. Little by little, though, what starts as a no-strings-attached fling evolves into something much deeper. Can they heal their emotional wounds to start afresh, or will the ghosts of relationships past haunt them forever?

Don't miss the third edition of the
***Bride Mountain** trilogy!*

Available now from the
Bride Mountain trilogy by Gina Wilkins:
MATCHED BY MOONLIGHT
A PROPOSAL AT THE WEDDING

HSE65814